THE LIGHT ON THE ISLAND

THE
LIGHT ON THE
ISLAND

TALES OF A LIGHTHOUSE KEEPER'S
FAMILY IN THE SAN JUAN ISLANDS

HELENE GLIDDEN

Foreword & Postscript by
MICHAEL D. McCLOSKEY

SAN JUAN
PUBLISHING

Published by
San Juan Publishing
P.O. Box 923
Woodinville, WA 98072
425-485-2813
sanjuanbooks@yahoo.com

The Light on the Island, ©1951 by Helene Glidden
Pacific Coast Seafood Chef, ©1953 by Helene Glidden
Foreword and postscript, ©2001 by Michael D. McCloskey

First edition 1951 by Coward-McCann, Inc. New York, NY
Second edition by San Juan Publishing, Woodinville, WA
    First printing 2001; Second printing 2002; Third printing 2003;
    Fourth printing 2010; Fifth printing 2015

Printed in Canada

Design and Cartography: Jennifer LaRock Shontz
Proofreader: Sherrill Carlson

Front cover illustration: *The lighthouse on Patos Island.* Illustration by
    Jennifer LaRock Shontz
Back cover photograph: *Looking southeast between Patos Island (left) and
    Little Patos Island (right), the sun rises on New Year's morning in 1999.*
    Photo by Michael D. McCloskey
Frontispiece: *Patos Island Lighthouse and keeper's residence on Alden Point,
    circa 1940.* Photo courtesy of Coast Guard Museum Northwest

ISBN 0-9707399-0-7

Library of Congress Catalog Card Number: 2001 126019

CONTENTS

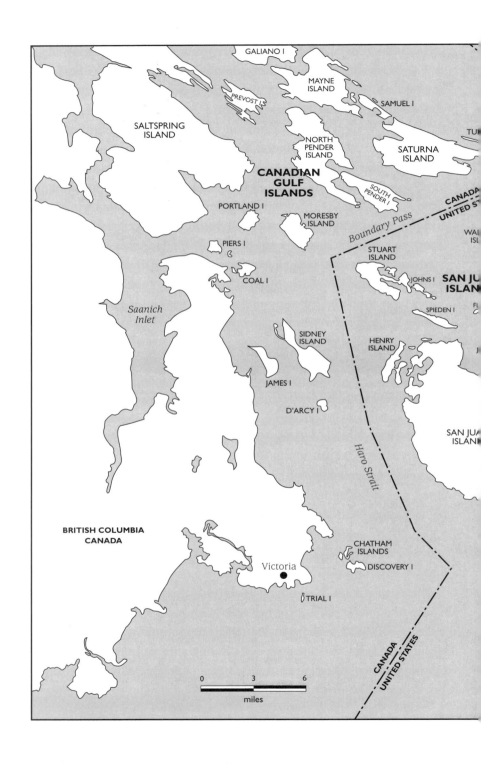

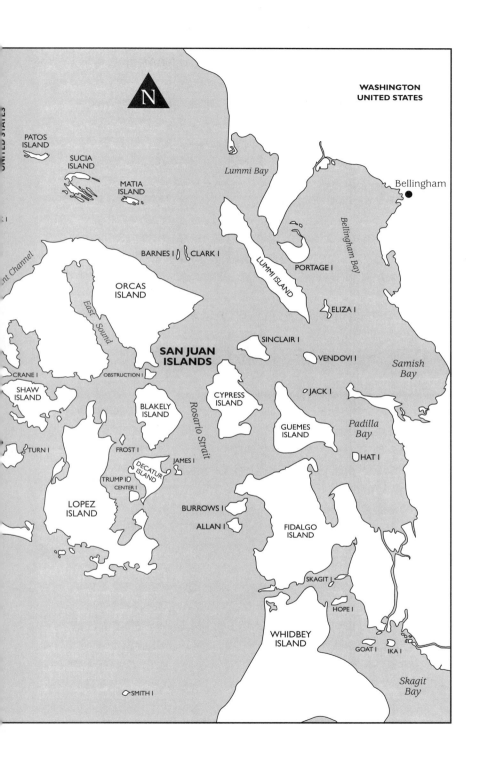

ACKNOWLEDGMENTS

Deborah Bagg, Woodinville Library
Sherrill Carlson, Proofreader
Coast Guard Museum Northwest, Pier 36, Seattle
Capt. E.L. Davis
Tom Doyle
Larry Dubia
James A. Gibbs, author
Jane Lowrey, Bellingham Public Library
Lucile S. McDonald, author
Sharlene and Ted Nelson, authors of *Umbrella Guide to Washington Lighthouses* and *Umbrella Guide to Oregon Lighthouses*, Epicenter Press, Kenmore, WA
New Dungeness Chapter, U.S. Lighthouse Society
Tom Pardee, captain of the *Sea Rat*
Puget Sound Maritime Historical Society
Roche Harbor Resort
Jennifer LaRock Shontz, Red Shoe Design, Seattle, WA
Kent Sturgis, President/Publisher, Epicenter Press, Kenmore, WA

FOREWORD

Helene Glidden's classic, *The Light on the Island*, chronicles the life of a lighthouse keeper's family on Patos Island from 1905–1913. Helene, or "Angie" as she calls herself in the story, records the hardships, adventures and heroism her family experienced in this remote corner of Washington State's San Juan Islands.

Angie combines the innocent charm of Shirley Temple with the adventurous spirit of Mark Twain's Huckleberry Finn as she narrates a tale that begins with the five-year-old and her family moving to Patos. Her father reluctantly agrees to the move in order to provide shelter for his wife and thirteen children.

The Light on the Island was originally published on October 15, 1951. This 50th Anniversary Edition contains a postscript with photos and biographical information about Helene's family. It also includes four additional stories about "Angie" from Mrs. Glidden's 1953 cookbook, *Pacific Coast Seafood Chef*.

Today, *The Light on the Island* preserves an important era of light-house life along with an historical period of the San Juan Islands. Readers can once again enjoy Helene Glidden's sense of humor and unique story telling abilities.

Michael McCloskey
Henry Island
March, 2001

The lighthouse on Patos Island as it appeared in 1999. *Photo by Michael D. McCloskey*

Patos Island with Active Cove and Little Patos on the right. Sucia Island is in the distance at the top of the photo. *Photo courtesy of Coast Guard Museum Northwest*

CHAPTER ONE

66 "D amn-it-to-hell," roared Papa. "I won't go back to Patos Island!"

His loud voice raised goose pimples on my arms. I pulled my legs up and rested my chin on my knees—and tried to avoid Mamma's long party dress as it slapped against my face. I knew it was wrong to be hiding in Mamma's closet. On several occasions I had been punished for eavesdropping.

The clothes closet wasn't really a closet in the strict sense of the word. It was merely two curtains hung on a pole across the end of Mamma's bedroom. The pile of blankets on which I always sat or reclined was comfortable, and often I would fall asleep, listening to the soft drone of Mamma's voice.

"You can't make me go back!" continued Papa.

I peeked out through the crack in the curtains, pushing Mamma's party dress out of my face again.

Mamma was lying in bed with the newest twin boys, Laurel and Noel, resting on her breast. She stroked the babies' heads as she answered Papa.

"Now, Ed, you know full well that we can't continue to live in the manner we are living. I'm ashamed to poke my face outside this house, the way folks are talking."

"Let them talk!" snapped Papa. "They can't drive me away from my good job, and the chance of a lifetime to make good, just because we have thirteen children. A silly thing to run away from a town just because the neighbors think thirteen children are a disgrace. I won't go. I won't." Papa waved his short arms, and his small hands flip-flapped about pitifully.

Papa was a fiery little Frenchman; his hands often conveyed more of his thoughts than his speech brought out. "Tie Papa's dainty little hands behind his back," said Mamma, "and you can only half understand what he's talking about."

I watched Papa's dainty little hands now, as they settled to stroke Mamma's long shining hair, "So soft—so smooth," he cooed, sinking down on the edge of the bed.

Papa was a handsome man. His black curly hair was carefully parted in the center and brushed back over his beautifully formed ears. His eyes, with their black curling lashes, were large and dark brown. When he sat on the bed, you couldn't notice how short he was. He looked tall and strong.

"Papa would have been a tall man," Mamma once told us, "only his legs were injured when he was seventeen. He was caught in a log jam on the Hudson River."

Papa's one bad habit was his swearing. Whenever Mamma spoke to him about his profanity, he would flare up in anger, "Hell, I don't swear—damn it."

"He honestly doesn't know that he is swearing," explained Mamma. "It's the only language he knows. He picked it up on the Hudson when he was a logger."

Papa's hand slid down to fumble with the buttons on Mamma's dress.

"Now Ed," she scolded. "Don't start that again—mid-morning is not the time for love making. I have to finish nursing these babies and get to work for your other eleven offspring. I'd think you'd get tired of all this foolishness. Thirteen children are enough!"

Mamma looked pretty when she was mad at Papa. Her blue eyes snapped, and her otherwise quiet face came to life with fire and color. Mamma was a tall blonde woman, quiet in her ways. "English, and cold blooded," Papa used to say about her. "Doesn't know how to love like a French girl."

"Who wants to love like a French girl?" Mamma would ask. "I don't need to . . . . "

"Stop it!" ordered Mamma. "And go about your business." I gave Mamma's party dress a slap, so I could see past it. I wanted to see what Papa was doing to Mamma. The party dress fell down on my head with a loud swish and crackle of taffeta. As I fought to free myself of its folds, Papa grabbed my arm.

"Eavesdropping again!" he shouted.

"No, sir," I answered, "just listening."

"Listening is eavesdropping," said Mamma. "Especially because you tell everything you hear to the neighbors, and that is one reason they're all laughing at us."

"They don't laugh at you," I explained. "They just feel sorry for all of us. Yesterday Mrs. Arnold said, 'I feel so sorry for that poor Mrs. LaBrege and all those poor little youngsters. She tries so hard to make ends meet—and that handsome, no-good husband of hers—he spends his time shouting at the babies and winking at all the pretty girls.'"

"*Who* said that?" shouted Papa. He grabbed my arm, and I began to cry.

"Mrs. Arnold did—and Mrs. Baxter said, 'Oh, he's all right. He works hard, but his job doesn't pay enough. It is sort of a pitiful set-up.'"

"Hell," swore Papa, "who do they think they are? I make as much as either of their husbands do."

"Yes, but they only have one child apiece," answered Mamma. "You can see that to save our self-respect we must go back to Patos Island."

"Patos—Patos," groaned Papa, "that godforsaken island, with its ever blinking light and lonely, groaning fog signal. I'm not cut out to be a lighthouse keeper. I like dances, parties, friends. I like my lodge; I'm going up in the Masons. *And* I like my job as customs officer. Look, Estelle—" Papa was pleading now, "I'm figuring out a way for us. I'm a good shoe cobbler. I figure that if I catch Spanish John, I can take the reward money and set up a shoestore. Make fancy shoes."

"Spanish John—" sneered Mamma. "Slim chance you have of catching Spanish John. Why, he has eluded the smartest of the Coast Guardsmen. No one has ever come near enough to him even to tell what he looks like."

Papa got an envelope from the top bureau drawer and pulled a newspaper out of it. "Look here," he said.

Mamma read: "Spanish John Seen Near Canadian Border— White Sloop Eludes U.S. Revenue Cutter Guard." And across the sheet was printed a picture of Spanish John.

"He has such lovely eyes," sighed Mamma. "I can't believe he's a killer."

"He's not a killer," said Papa. "He's the head of a ring of opium smugglers, operating through the San Juan Islands into Canada. There's a thousand-dollar reward for his capture, and I know a good Chinese who knows Spanish John. I did him a good turn down at the customs last month. I helped him get some imports through. He offered to help me locate Spanish John. So you see, Estelle, I can't leave now. I can't go to Patos Island."

"Ed LaBrege!" Mamma got up from the bed. "You *will* go to Patos Island! I have already written to the proper authorities and you have your old job back. At Patos we had everything we wanted to eat. Free gardens, free wood, free coal, free housing, free every-thing. We can have cows, chickens—just as we had before. We can save most of your salary. And our children will grow up with self-respect."

"No," wailed Papa. "I spent five years on Patos Island. It was like being in prison. Send back the appointment. I can't go there again—" He put his arms around Mamma and drew her back to the bed, and began to coo to her in his best Frenchy love-way. "Now, *ma petite,* let me convince you."

He pressed his lips to Mamma's, and tipped her over on the bed.

"Are we going to Patos Island?" I asked in a loud voice.

Papa jumped up. "You get out of here," he roared, slapping me on the back of the dress.

I ran out, shouting to my brothers and sisters as I rushed through the kitchen, parlor, and two upstairs bedrooms. "We're going to move to Patos Island, and have chickens, and free cows."

From past experience I knew that Mamma would have her way. She always talked Papa down in an argument. I ran out of doors and to every neighbor's house, shouting the news. "We're going to Patos Island so you can't talk about us and feel sorry for us any more."

After I had informed the neighbors I rushed home. I heard Papa shouting. Stealthily I crept beneath the window and stood listening.

"All right, I'll go. I'd go to hell for you. That's what a man is in for when he loves a woman. I'll *go* to Patos, but if things go wrong, I'm giving you warning I'll leave. Even if I have to lose you and the children, I'll *leave*."

Calm was Mamma's answer, "I'll take that chance." I went inside where the kids were standing around, looking scared. They were always upset when Papa and Mamma quarreled. The fighting didn't bother me, because I hung around Papa more than the others did, and saw through his sham. Deep in his heart, down under the shouting, swearing, and threats of spankings, he was kind and loving.

"What's going on in the bedroom?" asked my ten-year-old sister Estelle and my brother Roy, who was fourteen.

"Papa don't want to go to Patos and Mamma is making him go—and we're all going to move there."

"Gosh, no!" breathed Roy. "That godforsaken place?"

"What's Patos?" asked Lynn and René. They were seven and six years old, and didn't like the idea of my knowing anything they didn't, because I was only five. "It's an island in the San Juans," answered Estelle. "Papa was lighthouse keeper there before you were born."

"So lonesome," said Roy, "and so quiet that when the foghorn blows it rattles your teeth until they ache. The nights are the worst; then the loons cry. I used to duck under the covers, I was so scared. Papa always carried a gun in the daytime, and slept with it under his pillow at night; there were so many smugglers hanging around. I don't want to go back to Patos. I'm on Papa's side."

"I want to go," said Estelle. "Mamma has often told me about it. It's a historical landmark in Georgia Straits, on the edge of Puget Sound. When Captain Prevost was surveying the San Juan Islands for Great Britain, he anchored Her Majesty's Ship *Satellite* off Patos Island. His surveyor's stone is still there. I want to go."

Mary came downstairs. She had been attending the three-year-old twins, Edmund and Elizabeth, and two-year-old Thalia. Mary was nineteen, and a recent bride. Her husband was Capt. Alexander Clark from nearby Fort Worden.

"What's going on?" she asked. "I heard Papa shouting."

"Mamma is making Papa go back to Patos," answered Roy. "That lousy, godforsaken island!"

"Oh, that," said Mary. "I knew about the plan weeks ago. I think it's a grand idea. I'm going too; Al is appointed assistant keeper. We'll live in the other side of the house."

"I'm on Papa's side," declared Clara, my eleven-year-old sister. "I don't want to go to that lonely place."

"We can have fun at Patos," answered Mary. "It's a beautiful place. I love it!"

"Love it?" shouted Roy. "What's there to love?"

"Oh, the beaches, the woods, the sunsets. Don't you remember the fun we had on the beaches? But no, you were so young when we left there. I guess you don't remember anything except that you didn't have any boys to play with."

Papa came out of the bedroom, followed by Mamma. "Oh, Papa, I'm so thrilled!" squealed Mary.

"Don't be so happy about my misfortune," he answered. He took his cap from the hook and went out without saying good-bye.

"I don't blame Papa for being mad," stormed Clara. "Poking him off on a dreary island. I'm on his side."

"There'll be no sides!" Mamma spoke with authority. "We're going to Patos Island!"

We were accustomed to Mamma making the final decisions in all family matters, because Papa refused to learn to read or write in English.

"I read and write in French," he said. "If I learn to do so in English, Mamma would force me to do all the bookwork and keep the accounts. Besides, she'd stop reading to me. I love Mamma's voice."

The only sad part of leaving Port Townsend was when Mamma brought my four-year-old sister Margaret home from Grandma's. Margaret had never been strong. She required special care that Mamma was unable to give her. Grandma Lee had taken her when she was a small baby.

At first, Margaret wept constantly, calling for Grandma. Finally, succumbing to the charms of Edmund and Elizabeth, she accepted the change and seemed quite content.

Two weeks dragged by, and finally on August 15, 1905, we locked the door of the little brown house and walked to the docks. The fishing boat that Papa had hired looked dirty and not a bit thrilling. We were finally aboard and on our way to Patos—Mamma and Mary and Estelle and I who wanted to go, and Papa, Roy, and all the rest of the kids who didn't want to go.

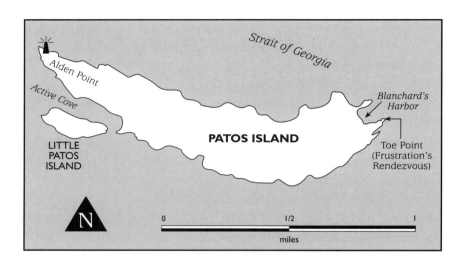

Strait of Georgia

Alden Point

Active Cove

LITTLE
PATOS
ISLAND

PATOS ISLAND

Blanchard's
Harbor

Toe Point
(Frustration's
Rendezvous)

N

0   1/2   1

miles

CHAPTER TWO

You can sit back here," said Papa. He indicated some mounds on the afterdeck. "These tarps are *clean*."

"They don't look clean." Mamma was dubious. "Those tarps are clean!" repeated Papa. "I helped the men spread them over the fish nets this morning." He grabbed me by the arm and sat me down on one of the piles. Lynn and René promptly climbed up beside me.

"Oh, all right," sighed Mamma. She sat on the tarp, Margaret and Thalia on her lap, and pulled the perambulator with the sleeping twins in it up close beside her. Mary took charge of Edmund and Elizabeth. Estelle and Clara arranged their skirts over another mound of fish nets, and sat smirking at the young deckhands.

"Behave yourselves!" Mamma's voice was peremptory.

"Why, Mamma," said Estelle with hurt accusation in her voice, "we weren't doing anything."

"Quiet!" ordered Papa. "You were trying to attract the attention of those boys—seems to me you're awfully young to be flirting."

"Papa—we weren't—" Clara began.

"Be quiet!" Papa barked again.

Roy and Al wandered forward. "I want to look the boat over," Al said.

"Well-there goes my last chance to catch Spanish John,"Papa sighed as he watched Port Townsend fade away in the distance.

"Good-bye to all our poverty and misery." Mamma's eyes were radiant.

We took the inland route from Admiralty Inlet out to Rosario Strait, past Lopez Island and Fidalgo. We stopped at Decatur Island Lighthouse to say good-bye to the keeper and his family. The hours sped by; it was evening before we reached Cypress and quite dark when we passed Orcas and Lummi.

Mamma had put the smaller children to bed below. "Come now," she said to Lynn, René, and me, "you must go down and get some sleep."

"I don't want to sleep," I cried. "I want to see the stars and listen to the water."

"Go below!" ordered Papa. We went reluctantly.

The hold stank of past cargoes of fish, combined with burned gas and babies' diapers. In a short time we were all very seasick. In the darkness I found the ladder and climbed to the deck. Staggering to a pile of fish nets, I lay face down and succumbed to my wretchedness.

Day was breaking when I heard Papa shouting, "Come and look. There she is!" At the sound of running feet, I pulled myself up from the tarp. There was Patos!

"Oh, it's a beautiful island!" I exclaimed. "All green and brown trees. And look at the sparkling white beach at her skirts."

"Her skirts?" asked Lynn. "Whose skirts?"

"Why, Patos'," I answered. "She's wearing a green hat and waist, and her skirts are all brown where the sun scorched the grass, and her white petticoat shows where the beach is."

"Oh, dry up!" said Roy. "Such nonsense!"

But I didn't mind my brothers. They were only boys and didn't understand such things. I gazed and gazed at lovely Patos, and as the boat drew nearer I thought I saw Patos wave to me and smile.

"She waved!" I whispered to Mamma.

"She didn't *really*," Mamma explained. "You probably saw a tree waving, and some Spanish moss that shook in the wind and looked like a smile."

"She waved," I insisted, "and I waved back."

The boat fought her way through a turbulent passage and skidded to a standstill like a puppy on a highly polished floor. She came to rest in the middle of the Bay, a still-water cove formed by Patos proper and Little Patos, an adjoining small island. There being no landing, we climbed down a steep ladder into a small skiff and were rowed to the beach.

When we were all ashore, we followed Papa up a flight of stairs and along a boardwalk that led off through the trees. We must have presented a laughable sight to anyone who might have been watching; our clothing was so wrinkled and soiled.

We followed Papa through the trees, past a fenced-in field where bellowed a large Holstein bull; past a series of gardens and a chicken house; orchard; barn. We opened a large whitewashed gate and continued downhill to a beautiful large white house with a red roof, beyond which, like a sentinel, loomed the lighthouse. We were ushered into the house by the keeper of the light; the man whose place Papa had come to take.

In a few days, our furniture arrived, and we were comfortably settled. The large duplex house seemed enormous after our small crowded place in Port Townsend. Across the front was a large veranda that commanded a full view of the Straits of Georgia.

I enjoyed watching the ships pass by; four-masted sailing ships with all sails set, being towed out past Cape Flattery to the ocean by chugging little tugs. Sometimes the hawser would break, and while the large schooner waltzed clumsily in the whirlpools off Patos Point, the little tug stood patiently by and waited for a chance to catch her wayward charge.

My favorite ship was the snow-white Canadian steamer *Princess Charlotte*. She passed Patos daily at dusk, her lights blinking like fairy lanterns.

"She's a *phantom* ship," said Estelle. "You can hear her breath searing the water as she passes by."

"Aw, shucks," answered Roy. "That noise is her bilge water running out."

Mamma didn't waste any time in getting our schooling started. On her first trip to Bellingham, she bought the necessary current textbooks.

"We'll hold school in the dining room," she said. "I think it would be best to teach Clara, Estelle, and Roy in the morning, and Lynn and René during the afternoon."

"I don't want to be taught," Lynn's blue eyes were rebellious. "I don't like school."

"Be quiet!" shouted Papa. "Everyone likes school. Do you want to grow up to be a dummy?"

"Like you?" asked Lynn. Mamma turned her face away to hide a smile, but she was loyal to Papa.

"Your papa is a very well-educated man," she said.

"But he didn't go to school," insisted Lynn. "You said so once."

"He learned things the hard way," explained Mamma.

"I want to learn things the hard way. I don't want to go to school—"

"That's just what you're going to do," said Papa. He turned Lynn over his knee and spanked him soundly. "This is the hard way," he said. "You'll go to school and be quiet about it!"

I sat on a couch in the dining room and watched and listened until Mamma discovered that I excelled the boys in their studies. Thus at five I became one of Mamma's pupils.

Mamma and Papa organized a Saturday evening discussion club. "In order to teach you the fundamentals of democracy," Papa explained. "Bring your troubles to the club each week, and we'll iron them out together." It was because of this club that we children learned at an early age that there are no *rights* without the accompanying *obligations*.

"We should have a Sunday school," Al announced one evening when we were all together for dinner. "I'll go to town and get the materials. These kids are quite the little heathens."

"A splendid idea!" agreed Mamma. "Will you conduct the classes?"

Al had been a chaplain in the army during the Spanish-American War. He readily accepted the responsibility of our religious education. At first the Sunday school idea didn't find favor with Lynn, René, and me. We liked to be up early and away exploring the island. Sundays to us were no different from any other day. Papa often had to hunt for us when Sunday school time approached. I remember one particular Sunday when we were investigating a dead seal that had been left on the rocks by the night tide. Papa surprised us and began to switch our legs, shouting, "You god-damn kids get up there to Sunday school. Hell! Do you want to grow up to be god-damn heathens?"

Al proved to be a capable teacher. Before long we were looking forward to our meetings on Sunday. I liked the singing best. One song I shall always remember, "Love Lifted Me." For a long time I thought the grownups were singing "Come little bee." I was fascinated with the words, "When nothing else will help, Come little bee." I used to wonder what sort of help a bee had to offer.

My first trip from Patos was to Bellingham. Papa himself had gone to Bellingham before, but, as the boat accommodated only five persons, Clara, Estelle, and Roy had gone with him. Now Lynn, René, Mamma, and I were going.

"Look out!" yelled Papa. I ducked my head just in time to avoid being hit by the boom.

"Damn-it-to-hell!" Papa scowled as he swore. "Can't you keep your head out of the way of that god-damn stick? Sit lower in the boat!"

"Must you swear so?" asked Mamma. "I think the children understand plain English."

"Damn-it, I wasn't swearing!" said Papa. "This goddamn trip to Bellingham every month is going to kill me off. Twenty-five miles in this god-damn rowboat. My arms ache, my back aches, and something else aches and it's not this hard seat."

"Ed!" Mamma's admonishing exclamation did no good; Papa kept on talking.

"And you accuse me of swearing. Did you ever row a boat from Patos to Bellingham? Did you ever cross this god-damn Bellingham Bay with a cantankerous sail flapping the wrong way, and a damned kid forever getting her head in the way of the boom? God-damn-it, don't accuse me of swearing. I *don't* swear!"

"Why don't you lower the sails; they're doing you no good." Mamma was angry now. "You knew the wind was wrong for sailing when we left Lummi."

"Hell, how can a man row the boat and furl the sails at the same time? I haven't got four hands."

"Hold the rudder, Lynn!" said Mamma. Lynn grabbed the stick and held fast. Mamma worked swiftly, and in a few minutes the sails were down.

"Give me an oar," said Mamma. She seated herself beside Papa, and together they battled the tide into Bellingham.

"Whew!" said Papa, when he had tied the boat to the float. "I hope the wind and tide favor us when we go home. That was the toughest gale I ever rowed out. I wish-to-hell I'd never seen that godforsaken island. It'll be the death of me yet!"

"In a sense the island is God forsaken," Mamma answered. "Not because God has forsaken it, but because apparently the master of the island has forsaken God."

"What the hell do you mean?" asked Papa. "I believe in God as much as you do." He began to climb up the ramp to the dock, muttering, "Forsaken God! Hell!"

"Watch your language!" called Mamma.

"Jesus Christ, what for? I wasn't swearing."

It was noon the following day before Papa and Mamma finished their shopping and started home. The boat was loaded with a month's supply of groceries.

"This is the last time," announced Papa.

"For what?" asked Mamma.

"For rowing to Bellingham."

"How do you propose to get our supplies?"

"We'll trade at the mercantile at East Sound."

Mamma was thoughtful. "Ed, I think I'll write in to headquarters and ask for a motor boat for Patos. We really need one."

"You could write," said Papa, "but it probably won't do any good. We tried to get one years ago, and the request was turned down."

"Just the same, I'm going to try," answered Mamma.

"There's a squall coming." Papa was worried. "I hope we make Lummi before it blows."

The storm hit when we were a few miles out of Bellingham. Our boat was tossed about like a matchbox. Mamma held the rudder stick while Papa struggled with the oars. He was sweating profusely and swearing under his breath. I felt sorry for Papa. The muscles in his neck stood out in ridges, and he wheezed with every lunge of the oars. He stood up so he could put more weight on the oars.

"Get down in the bottom of the boat!" he ordered us. Lynn, René, and I quickly obeyed. We were frightened by the plunging of the boat as it climbed the huge swells and dropped with a sickening slap in the trough before climbing another wave.

"Can she ride it out?" asked Mamma. Her face was white.

"We'll have to unload!" shouted Papa. "You kids get on your knees and start throwing the groceries overboard. Don't stand up— you'll be washed overboard."

We hastened to obey. Boxes of crackers, oatmeal, sugar, and flour were swallowed up by the dark green monstrous waves. I began to cry.

"Shut up that bawling. Everything's all right!" shouted Papa. "I've ridden out worse storms than this in this same lifeboat."

I looked at Mamma for reassurance. Her mouth was pressed into a tight line. Her eyes were closed. Her hands were white on the rudder stick. I began to cry again.

"Shut up, Angel!" said Lynn. "You'll wreck this god-damn boat!" It was the first time Lynn had ever sworn. I was so amazed that I stopped crying. Night suddenly swooped down, enveloping us in her black wings.

The boat continued to toss, lunge, roll, and spank in the trough for several hours. Suddenly I felt an awful shudder go through her.

"She's struck bottom!" said Papa. "Where, I don't know!"

"It must be Lummi Island," said Mamma. She peered around into the inky darkness.

"There's a light!" shouted Papa. "Yell—everyone yell." He began, "Yooooo!" and we all joined in, "Help—help!" We shouted for a long time before we saw lanterns bobbing on shore.

"Thank God!" said Papa. Lynn held the rudder stick while Mamma waved our lantern above her head.

Before long, a large launch appeared. As it drew near our boat, Papa left his oars, and tossed our painter to reaching hands aboard the launch.

When we were safely ashore I began to cry in earnest. I was joined by Lynn and René.

We were hurried up the beach and into a cabin, a smelly, dirty place, but warm and safe. I couldn't stop crying. Someone began to pull my clothes off. I looked at Lynn and René. They were being undressed also. I stopped crying. I no longer cared what happened.

It was morning when I woke up. Something was tickling my arm. I discovered that it was covered with little white worms. Mamma was sitting on a stump near the cabin door.

"Look, Mamma," I said, "I'm all wormy."

She crossed to where I lay. "Good gracious," she whispered, "that mattress is full of maggots."

She lifted me up and pulled me outside. "Your clothes are dry. Put them on."

We had been rescued by a party of Indians who were camped on the beach.

I finished dressing and started in search of Papa. He was sitting on the beach, completely surrounded by Indians. I timidly ran up and sat on his knee.

"Good papoose," one of the Indians remarked.

"She's the best damned youngster I own," agreed Papa. "She's the only one who's not afraid of me." I snuggled up against him.

"You see Blanchard? You see Spaniss John?" asked the largest and darkest of the Indians.

"Blanchard? He's at Patos," answered Papa. "But what about Spanish John. Do you know him? Where is he?" Papa stood up in his excitement.

"Long time he no come," answered the Indian. "He come with Blanchard all time—he no come many long time."

"With Blanchard! Are you sure?" asked Papa. The Indian nodded his head.

Mr. Blanchard was an old historian who lived at the far end of Patos Island. He built the old log cabin in which he lived, many years before the island was declared a government reservation.

"He thinks he owns Patos," Papa once said, "so I let him stay, even though it's against regulations. Anyone who'd remain on Patos for sixty years, as he has, should be given the damned place."

"I have to be shoving off." Papa thanked the Indians for their hospitality and kindness to us. He ran all the way to the boat. I had never seen him quite so excited.

"Hurry up and get in," he ordered Mamma. "I have to get home and talk to Blanchard."

"We have to stop at East Sound for groceries," Mamma reminded him, when we were again on our way.

The weather was favorable for sailing. We reached Orcas Island early in the afternoon. Papa bought a supply of food. In a short time, we were on our way home. As we neared Patos, Lynn began to scratch.

"Mamma, I itch," he complained.

"Where?" asked Mamma.

"On my head, most," he answered, "but all over *some*."

"I itch too," said René.

"Well, I tickle," I said.

Mamma looked at Lynn's head. "Oh, for heaven's sake! *Lice!*"

"Fleas, too!" said Papa. He began to scratch.

"I shouldn't wonder," said Mamma. "That cabin was *filthy!*"

A few days later Lynn and I broke out with the itch between our fingers.

"Perhaps we should have been better off if we had drowned," said Mamma, as she spread our hands with sulphur and lard.

Poor Mamma! All thirteen children caught the itch! Before she was through with the ordeal, she hated the word "Indian."

I went with Papa to Blanchard's Harbor. Mr. Blanchard was sitting on a nail keg outside his cabin door.

"Hello!" he greeted us. His snow-white beard bobbed. "Nice to see you, Ed. You don't get down here as much as you used to twenty years ago."

"I didn't have thirteen youngsters then. My family keeps me humping these days."

Mr. Blanchard brought a bench from the cabin. "Sit down. What's the news?"

"Not much," answered Papa. "We were shipwrecked on Lummi, near the Indian reservation a few nights ago. Bunch of Siwashes rescued us. Lost about fifty dollars' worth of groceries."

"You don't say!" sympathized Mr. Blanchard. "Funny thing happened," Papa said. "One of the bucks asked about you. Said you were over there with Spanish John some time ago."

"Spanish John! With me? You're joking."

"That's what he said. I just wondered," said Papa.

Mr. Blanchard looked out over the harbor. After a while he said, "Ed, you've known me for a long time. I'd hate to break off our friendship; but if you're insinuating that I'm in league with those opium smugglers, I'll have to bid you good-bye."

"No such thing," said Papa. "Only if you know anything about Spanish John, I'd like to hear it. I could use that reward money."

"That kind of money brings no happiness to anyone. Blood money is always damned."

"Well, I'll be going," said Papa. "Have a lot to do before sundown."

We started down the trail. Mr. Blanchard called after us.

"Ed, did you ever know a truthful Siwash?"

"I don't remember any," Papa shouted. He mumbled, "Damned funny incident."

"What?" I asked. "What's damned funny?"

"You stop that god-damn swearing," he said.

Summer lingered late that first year on Patos. In September Papa decided to teach us to swim.

"You'll be racing all over the island, and God knows there's plenty of danger," he explained. "Slippery rocks, icy paths, and before long you'll want to take the boat out alone. You'll have to learn to swim right away."

He made a wide belt of canvas, which he fastened about our middles. A rope was securely tied to the belt at the back. Then he dipped us one at a time into the water.

"Swim or sink!" he said.

Lynn, who was first, began to swim almost at once. Papa held the rope tight until he was satisfied that Lynn had mastered the correct motions. Then he lowered him into the deep water. Lynn had no fear of the water. When he was six, he had been tied to a tree stump and set adrift, by his playmates. It was several hours before he was rescued. The frightening ordeal might have caused a more timid child to fear the water; it simply caused Lynn to be fascinated by the sea.

When René's turn came to be lowered into the bay, he cried out, "No, no, Papa! I don't want to swim." He squirmed and tried to pull away.

"God-damn-it, you'll learn or get drowned!" Papa lowered him into the deep pool. René sank to the bottom at once. When Papa pulled him up he was coughing and sputtering.

"Swim, damn-it!" yelled Papa. René didn't move.

"Down you go!" roared Papa. He lowered the rope.

"Stop it!"

Papa turned around to see who was daring to give him orders. It was Al.

"Hell," said Papa, "he's got to learn to swim."

"He's drowning, you damn fool!" shouted Al. He snatched the rope from Papa's hands, and pulled René out. "He's about done in," he said, kneeling over René. "That's the cruelest way to teach a kid to swim I've ever seen."

Papa was so astonished that Al should question his motives that he just stood there with his mouth open.

"Don't *ever, anytime,* try to teach these kids to swim again!" said Al. "I'll do it myself."

"That's the way I learned," Papa protested. "I was dropped in the Hudson River."

"I wonder what Mother would say if she'd seen this little drama; this child's lungs are full of water. I doubt if he'll ever go in again. He's not very strong at his best."

"I guess we'd better not say anything about the incident to the women." Papa's voice was almost quiet—he who habitually yelled when he talked.

Al stood up and lifted René in his arms. "Dad, if you'll leave the swimming lessons to me in the future, I'll promise to forget this whole business."

"It's agreed," said Papa. "I wouldn't want to hurt one of the youngsters. I thought he'd have spunk enough to swim."

In a few days, with patience and kindness, Al taught Lynn and me to swim. René wouldn't be coaxed to try again.

"Now that you can swim," said Papa, "you can bring the cows home at night. Also, I'd like to have you cover the beaches occasionally and report to me what you find. That will save me a lot of walking."

Early the next morning Lynn, René, and I set out.

"The tide is in," said Lynn. "We'd better take the trail today; those rocks are damn slippery at high tide."

"You better quit that swearin'," said René.

"Why?"

"'Cause Mamma don't like swearin'."

"Papa swears; I'm goin' to be just like Papa."

"You better not let Mamma hear you swear."

"Hell sakes, she can't hear way down here. Keep still and walk a little faster. We hafta go clear around this island."

My legs were shorter than Lynn's and René's; they ran on ahead of me. It was then I saw a face in the woods. It looked straight at me and then disappeared.

"Lynn!" I shouted. I ran to catch up.

"What's the matter?" the boys asked.

"I saw a man—a man with long white hair. He was looking at me."

"By hell!" said Lynn. "Where was he?" We walked back to where I saw the face. "It was right in those trees," I said.

"Nobody's there," said Lynn. "Maybe you didn't see nothin'. Maybe it was just some of that white moss hangin' down."

"I *thought* I saw a man."

"Was it Mr. Blanchard?" asked René.

"No," I answered.

"You didn't see nobody." Lynn was cross. "You better quit sayin' you saw any old man. Papa told me I was the boss of you when we go out alone. I guess you better go home. You're too slow anyway."

"No," I cried. "I won't see no more old men. I guess I didn't, really."

When we came to Blanchard's Harbor, we stopped to see Mr. Blanchard. He was sitting on a bench outside his cabin door.

"Sit down and have a drink of water," he invited. "You look tired out." He went inside and got a dipper of water. We all three drank from it.

Lynn started to carry the dipper back into the cabin.

"Don't!" cried Mr. Blanchard. He hurriedly snatched the dipper. "Don't *ever* go into my cabin. You can visit me all you want, but I don't like anyone, especially children, snooping in my cabin— I write, and you're liable to lose my manuscript."

"I'm writing a history of the San Juan Islands," he said. "About how the Spaniards and Indians found them; how they were named and how they finally were given to the United States."

We were too young to appreciate his tales then, but as we grew older and learned to love Patos, we came to understand the romance of the San Juans.

"I'll show you something," he said. "Come out to the Point." The Point was overgrown with wild rose and scrub oak; it was almost impregnable. We followed the old man as he fought his way through to a clearing on the extreme end of the Point. Blanchard's Harbor lay below us, silent and brooding.

"This is Frustration's Rendezvous," he informed us. His eyes were sad and he gazed off into space as he talked. "These are the boys who left their homes in China. Some from choice; others were shanghaied. They were smuggled in to serve as cheap labor. Many of them ended up here, due to the Chinese Exclusion Act.

"I found the bodies on the beaches, hands and feet tied. They were tossed overboard by the smugglers when the revenue cutters got nosy."

Mr. Blanchard's eyes filled with tears. "I buried them here, beneath these oaks—sometimes three in a single grave. There are no names—no markers. Only the memory of an old man to tell of their frustrated hopes."

I didn't understand. I had had no experience with death, but I loved to listen to Mr. Blanchard. In later years, Frustration's Rendezvous was to hold a different meaning for me with its overwhelming truth. It was here, among the graves of the Chinese boys, that I cried in the agony of first heartbreak.

On our way home, we found an interesting tree that later we named Big Mad, because it was the largest madroña on Patos.

"It's my very own tree!" I declared. Often as I lay beneath its branches, I fancied it was whispering to me in a rasping tone; as it dropped leaves in my face, I imagined them to be caresses.

But Big Mad wasn't our only pet tree. We learned to love Singing

Cedar, so named because, when we swung on the branches, the tree sang in a creaking sort of way. There was Mr. Pitch, the big fir pine out of whose heart flowed a stream of balsam, just right for chewing. We always stopped and filled our mouths with the gum. Even today, I think it far superior to chewing gum.

One day, we accidentally set fire to Mr. Pitch, and Papa and Al had a fierce time getting the fire out. They had to chop him down and frantically dig a trench to keep the fire from burning the whole island. Luckily, it began to rain and everything turned out all right. But we wept over the death of Mr. Pitch. To punish us, Papa forced us to saw him up, all by ourselves.

We always carried a few crumbs and wheat in our pockets for Millie, the little mother mouse who lived in a stump behind the boat-house. She was very tame, and used to come at our call. Millie had so many babies we couldn't count them; she had even more children than Mamma, and sometimes we caught a tiny little gray mouse. Baby field mice are adorable. Mamma didn't like them, though, and would never allow us to keep one in the house.

We always stopped down by the spring to see our pet toad, a huge, warted creature as large as a man's head. He watched for us each morning, for we nearly always had a few bugs and flies for him. Puffy seemed to know us, and we thought he smiled a welcome. Papa said that, as far as he knew, Puffy had been in that spot for more than twenty years. Mamma warned us not to touch him or we would get warts. We petted Puffy and played with him for several years, but the warts didn't appear. Perhaps we were immune—or Puffy reserved his warts for his enemies. We didn't know.

We had other friends along the way. Certain trees at favorite resting places. It was beneath the branches of Old Pine we lay stretched out on sultry summer days. Here were no ants, which never approved of pine needles, and the fragrance was pleasant to our nostrils. We used to chew the long needles; they had a certain pungent taste.

View of Patos Island from the water. *Photo courtesy of Puget Sound Maritime Historical Society*

CHAPTER THREE

R oy, Clara, and Estelle amused themselves by rowing the boat around the island, exploring every beach and inlet; they collected rare shells and sea pigeons' eggs. The eggs were very colorful in their black, brown, and white contrasts. They removed the contents and strung the eggshells on fishline. They made quite a showing when stretched across the rafters of the barn.

Estelle was interested in history, especially the history of the San Juan Islands. She spent long hours listening to Mr. Blanchard tell about the early-day gun battles between the smugglers and government agents among the islands.

"Patos was always called The Spaniards' Retreat," he said. "It's near the channel, making it an ideal spot to duck in and hide when pursued. Most revenuers pass it by when they're looking for smugglers. It's so out-of-the-way—and so little—seems as if no one could hide on this island. Still, I know where there is a cabin that even your father doesn't know about. A cabin right here on Patos."

"Where?" asked Estelle.

"Oh, no use to tell now," said Mr. Blanchard. "Been no one near it for forty years or so. Have you seen the Indians' burying ground?"

"No," answered Estelle. "Mamma told us about it, but we've never found it."

"I'll show you."

Mr. Blanchard led Estelle to a clearing, not far from Blanchard's Harbor.

"These mounds," he pointed out, "are graves of the Indians who died here—I don't know how many hundreds of years ago."

"How can you be sure they're Indian graves?" asked Estelle.

"They've been dug up—some of them. They held Indian relics and other positive proof."

"I'm going to dig some up," said Estelle.

"I wouldn't!" warned Mr. Blanchard. "I've been told there's a curse on them."

Estelle enlisted the aid of Roy and Clara. Before the week was out they had uncovered a great many tomahawks and crude Indian tools.

"Five graves—we dug up five graves!" Roy was elated over the amount of their findings. "What's this, Mamma?" he asked. "Looks like a cucumber."

"That's a phallic stone," Mamma answered. "You wouldn't understand its meaning. The Indians who once lived on Patos were evidently from the Far East. They no doubt buried the phallic stone with their dead, hoping the soul of the dead would enter the stone, and so live forever. It's a pagan idea. They were called 'phallus worshipers.' If the stone was erect in the grave you dug up, it was a man—the recumbent, or lying-down stone means a woman was buried there."

November came blowing in on Patos one dark night. The cold breath of it chilled the very rocks; it laid low the late fall flowers and garden greens.

"Looks like a long hard winter ahead for us," predicted Papa. "I hope our supplies hold out until spring."

That first winter on the island was a long, disagreeable one. It was too stormy for Papa to row to East Sound. Luckily, Papa had stocked up well with hay, mash, and grain for the cows and chickens, so we had an abundance of meat, eggs, and dairy products. It was an easy matter to catch all the fish we could use, and wild ducks were plentiful. We didn't have enough flour, sugar, or vegetables though, and the mice got into our large box of oatmeal. Mamma fed it to the pigs. Then my baby sister, Thalia, made a wrong turn in the hallway one dark night, fumbled about in the dark, and, unable to locate the chamber mug, climbed into the large box of soda crackers and thoroughly soaked it.

The only touch we had with the outside world was when the *Heather,* the ship that serviced the lighthouse, called with government supplies. The *Heather* came once a month, bringing the lighthouse inspector, coal, oil, and other necessities, but groceries was not of her cargo.

Through the kindness of Clarence Sherman, the inspector, we were able to get enough flour for our needs. Mr. Sherman always brought us a treat. He soon became a very dear friend, and we looked forward with pleasure to his visits.

It wouldn't have been too bad, if smallpox hadn't broken out in the family. It began with Roy, and before long seven of the children were down with it.

"Those Indian graves," said Mamma. "I was afraid they'd catch something from digging up all those dead Indians."

"After all these years, you would hardly expect to catch a disease from those graves," said Papa. "They must be hundreds of years old."

"Nevertheless," said Mamma, "I believe that's where they caught the smallpox. Don't ever let them dig up any more—if they live to try it."

Somehow, Lynn, René, and I escaped the sickness, as did little Margaret and Thalia. Mary and Al lived in the other side of the duplex house, and they too were free from the disease. We moved in with them, and poor Mamma had to care for the seven sick youngsters alone. It was a good thing for her that she had studied medicine.

In spite of Mamma's wonderful nursing, three of the younger babies couldn't be saved. Mamma was handicapped. She had nothing but quinine with which to fight the disease, and Laurel, Edmund, and Elizabeth contracted pneumonia and died, only a few hours apart.

Papa made a box and painted it white. Mamma lined it with a beautiful silk Chinese robe that Papa had acquired while he was a customs officer at Port Townsend.

There lay the three babies, side by side in the box. Mary said they looked like three little dolls, just sleeping. We didn't see them. Papa put the box on the wheelbarrow. Followed by Mamma, Mary, and Al, he set out for the woods. When they were out of sight, Lynn, René, and I followed. We had been told to remain at home, but, being very curious children, we had no intention of obeying.

They followed a path through the woods to the south slope, and stopped under a beautiful manzanita. Al dug a grave, and Papa and he lowered the white box into it. Mamma, Papa, Al, and Mary joined hands and formed a circle around the grave. They closed their eyes and together repeated, "The Lord is my Shepherd, I shall not want—" Before they had finished, Lynn, René, and I were whispering it with them.

When they had finished praying, Papa held Mamma in his arms while Al sang this beautiful song:

> Tender Shepherd, Thou has stilled
> Now Thy little lambs' brief weeping;
> Ah, how peaceful, pale, and mild
> In their little bed they're sleeping!
> And no sigh of anguish sore
> Heaves their little bosoms more.

None of the grownups appeared to notice us; we became bold enough to go near, but before we could catch a glimpse of the babies, Papa had put the lid on and was nailing it down. There were tears in Mamma's eyes, but she wasn't weeping. I watched Lynn's tears falling.

"What are you crying for?" I asked. My only experience with death was when our cocker spaniel, Black Bonnet, died in Port Townsend. I hadn't formed any particular attachment for the babies; they had always seemed rather bothersome to me.

"I'm crying because Black Bonnet is in a box under the ground, just like our babies," answered Lynn.

"I'll cry too," I decided. "I'll cry for the babies." I wrinkled up my face, but I couldn't squeeze out a tear.

Papa and Al finished burying the babies. As Mamma began the walk home, everyone followed in complete silence.

Back home, I asked Mary, "Why didn't you and Mamma cry for our babies? Don't you love 'em?"

"Oh, Angie, please hush!" answered Mary. "Of course, we all loved the babies, but you were hiding there in the woods. We didn't want to frighten you. Besides, Mamma hasn't time to cry. She has to save her energy for the other sick children."

"When will the babies come out of the ground?" I asked. Mary sat down and took me in her arms.

"Angie, our dear little sisters and brother are never coming back. They will always stay with Jesus." Mary began to weep. Her sobs shook me, so I climbed down from her lap.

Walking around the house, I discovered Elizabeth's rag doll, lying wet and limp in the dripping of the rain barrel. I picked the doll up and tenderly put it on the porch. It was then that I understood little honey-haired Elizabeth would *never* return. Why, this little doll would miss her dreadfully. I ran to the barn and, face down in the hay, I sobbed, "Jesus—bring 'em back—bring 'em back!"

It was Al who found me. "Now, now," he crooned, "nothing is *that* bad!" He tenderly rocked me in his arms, and explained how beautiful death really was. "It's just going away in a golden dream boat," he said. "Of course, *everyone* comes back *sometime*. You must laugh and try to make Mamma happy. She'll miss the babies." For many months, in the still of the night, I left my bed to snuggle up to Mamma and comfort her when she cried out in her grief.

Winter, as though ashamed of the havoc she had wrought, gathered up her frosty garments and slipped quietly away. Spring just as quietly took her place on the island. While we slept, she spread her cloth of golden buttercups over field and meadow.

Papa sailed to Bellingham. From there, he took passage on a boat for Astoria and the headquarters of the lighthouse service. He made quite a fuss before he was assured that a motorboat would be provided for Patos Island.

Mamma was jubilant. "Now we can get to town without you having to row," she said to Papa.

"It all helps a little," answered Papa, "but it doesn't make up for what we've lost; I wish to God I'd never listened to you. This god-damn island will get us all. You just wait and see. I should have stayed in Port Townsend and hunted for Spanish John."

"Fiddlesticks!" said Mamma.

CHAPTER FOUR

With spring came the newly born—six wobbly-legged calves, an assortment of chicks, ducklings, and goslings. Mamma was grateful for the added work. "It helps me to forget," she said. The little grave under the manzanita was the only visible sign of the past winter's tragedy.

Before the April violets were withered, summer rushed in. Gracefully arranging her display of wild roses and scarlet currant, she settled her warm comfort over the island.

"It's picnic weather," announced Mary. Everyone agreed. On Sunday morning we carried our lunch baskets to the beach, beyond the boathouse.

We were enjoying our picnic lunch, when Al suddenly stood up. "Listen!" he said. Before we had time to accustom our ears to the change from noisy chatter to a listening attitude, a large launch hurled itself into the cove, through the treacherous tide at the Head-of-the-Bay. The launch glided to a stop at a point in the Bay directly opposite our picnic place, and her master threw out an anchor. We could plainly see her name, *Sea Pigeon*. The owner of the *Sea Pigeon* pulled in a small skiff, which was being towed behind the launch and, first putting a dog into the boat, climbed in himself and rowed to shore. Papa walked down to the water's edge to meet him.

The boat was beached. The man stood up and commanded his dog to "heel." He stepped out onto the beach.

"Hello, there," he said. "I'm Billy Coutts. I heard there was a new family on the island, and came over to pay my respects."

"Glad to see you," said Papa.

We all crowded around the visitor. He was a fine-looking young man, with blond curls and blue eyes. He presented each of us children with a gift of candy and a package of chewing gum.

The brown dog curled up at the feet of his master, and we couldn't get him to budge.

"He won't move until I tell him to relax," said the man. "All right, old boy," he said softly, "relax."

Instantly the curly dog was off and, picking up a stick, indicated that he wanted to play. Al took the stick and threw it; the dog retrieved it at once.

"He's well trained," said Al.

"He hunts and retrieves, both," said Billy. "My brother and I train dogs in California. Curly is a water spaniel, and very obedient." He then put the dog through his tricks for us. Curly played dead, rolled over, sat up, and spoke. He was a beautiful dog, with a shining coat of little brown curls as soft as silk. We had a lot of fun with him, and were sorry when Billy left.

Billy Coutts came often to the island after that, and took us to parties and picnics and dances on the other islands in the San Juan group. He fished around Patos that summer. After Papa and Al built a large smoke-house, Billy furnished enough salmon to fill it. Some of the salmon were called tyees, and weighed as much as sixty pounds.

Billy told us of his family, and of his home in California. He also told of his earlier life.

"I was born in States Point, Maine, to be followed in a year by my brother, Fred. Mother became homesick shortly after Fred was born, so we went back to Scotland.

"Several years later, we returned to the United States. My father helped to lay out the city of Seattle. He made many of the paving blocks for the streets.

"I enlisted in the Navy during the Spanish-American War, and was assigned to the battleship *Oregon*. After the war I went to Honolulu and worked on a sugar plantation. Tiring of that, I returned to the States and to my beloved San Juan Islands. To me this is the prettiest place in the world."

"Did you ever run across Spanish John when you fished these waters?" asked Papa.

"Spanish John used to tie up at Sucia a few years back. I saw quite a bit of him. He's a mysterious individual—always slipping out in the dark of night. I haven't seen or heard of him for a long time."

"If I could find his hideout," said Papa, "I'd turn him in. With the reward money I'd get off this damned island."

"Many men would like to have your setup, LaBrege," said Billy. "Here you can live like a millionaire, without his responsibilities. You have plenty of time to fish, cruise, and just be lazy. Why don't you take it easy? I'd forget about finding Spanish John. It can't be done."

"Why can't it?" asked Papa.

"Because I've tried. I've searched these waters for three years. He's disappeared completely."

One day after Billy had gone home, after visiting with us, I found Mary seated on the rocks gazing after the *Sea Pigeon*. There were tears in her eyes.

"Are you crying because Billy is going away?" I asked.

"Oh, Angie! No! Please, baby, don't ever tell anyone that I was crying. Promise?"

"I won't tell," I answered. "What *did* make you cry?"

"Only because the world is so beautiful, and sometimes I'm not happy," answered Mary. We watched the *Sea Pigeon* out of sight.

Then, one day, Billy announced that he was going back to California. He asked our permission to leave his launch with us until he should return. We were overjoyed when he gave us his dog, Curly. Curly soon became our friend and constant companion.

Patos was sun scorched through June and July. The grass was dry and straw colored.

"Years ago," said Papa, "I made a grass slide for Mary and Roy. It was on the hill back of the house. They had a lot of fun sliding on barrel staves."

"Make us one?" begged Lynn.

Papa looked at Mamma.

"Aren't they a little young?" asked Mamma. "It's a dangerous slope. It ends on the brink of a deep gulch, with jagged rocks below."

"I'll dig a trench," promised Papa, "wide enough to stop the sleds. I don't think they're too young; besides, they could slide only during high tide. If they go overboard when the tide's in, they won't be killed."

"Don't tempt the devil," said Mamma.

Papa made us a sled of barrel staves, and showed us how to make the hillside slippery. He dug a wide trench at the bottom of the hill.

"Try to stop your sled before it reaches this spot," he said, "and I don't think there'll be any danger."

Mamma inspected the slide. "I don't think the trench is quite wide enough," she said.

"I tried it," answered Papa. "It stops the sled."

Lynn, René, and I were delighted with our new pastime. We went sliding every day. Sometimes Curly raced down the hill after us until he was worn out.

"Take Margaret and Thalia for a ride," said Papa. "You can hold them on behind you."

"I'd rather they didn't," argued Mamma. "They might not be able to handle the extra weight. Why don't you make some real sleds for the little girls?"

Papa made two small sleds. Margaret's was blue, Thalia's red.

We didn't like the idea of teaching the younger girls to slide. Margaret was all right, but we heartily disliked Thalia. She was so demanding and cantankerous.

"Thoroughly spoiled," said Al. "She makes Margaret's life miserable."

Margaret was our pet. She was a beautiful child with her long golden curls and deep blue eyes. She possessed an angelic disposition, her main object in life being an ardent desire to please everyone.

How different was Thalia. She ruled Margaret with an iron hand. Thalia had a tempestuous nature. Papa used to call her Stormy. She used to roll in the grass and scream at the least provocation. Mamma always petted her after one of these demonstrations. She said, "Thalia must be protected from emotional upsets at all costs." So Mamma always punished whoever made Thalia cry. Consequently, we all heartily disliked Thalia, keeping out of her way as much as possible.

"My swed is the pwettiest," murmured Thalia.

"Mine's pretty, too," volunteered Margaret. "Mine's blue and white."

"*Mine's* bwue and white!" yelled Thalia.

"No, yours is red," coaxed Margaret, who didn't want to quarrel on this wonderful day of days. She was a big girl now; big enough to slide with the boys. She just couldn't bear it if Thalia should go into a tantrum and order her to take her home.

"Mine's bwue and white—mine's bwue and white," insisted Thalia, punctuating her assertions with vicious little kicks at Margaret's legs.

Margaret's blue eyes filled with tears, but she heroically held back any sound. Lynn, who had witnessed the little scene, grabbed Thalia by the hand.

"Come on, nuisance. If you don't shut up you'll go back home. Your sled is red. Do you hear me? RED."

To my great surprise, Thalia did not throw herself down, as usual, or cry. Grasping her sled rope firmly, she ran on ahead. As she passed Margaret, she gave her a vengeful look and whispered—"Bwue and white."

The slide was in excellent condition, just as slick as only a grass slide can be. The boys rode behind the babies and guided their sleds, teaching them to turn off at the trench. The small girls laughed and squealed with delight.

We were resting, after a long period of sledding, when we heard the familiar putt-putt, putt-putt of the service launch.

"Papa's home! Papa's coming into the bay!" Leaving the sleds, and forgetting all about our small charges, we went scampering to the boathouse. No one noticed Margaret trying to keep up with us, and none of us heard Thalia screaming, as she rolled on the ground.

We greeted Papa, and were well on our way home when we encountered Margaret on the boardwalk.

"Well," said Papa, "look who's big enough to come to meet Papa. Now, where have you left Thalia?"

"Cryin'," mournfully related Margaret. "She's cryin' in the grass. I'm big now—she's just little." She scornfully tossed her long curls.

Papa knew that, here and now, Margaret was declaring her independence from her tyrant sister.

When we were past the barn, we heard Curly barking excitedly. The sound came from the direction of the grass slide. Curly never barked unless for a good reason. Papa put down the box of groceries and ran to the hill. We followed.

From the hilltop we saw Curly running up and down the bank, looking for a way to get down to the rocks below. The sun was so bright that it cast a glare over the sea; at first we couldn't see anything.

Then Lynn spied it. "There it is, Papa," he shouted. "It's out by the kelp bed." Then he screamed, "Oh, Papa, it's Thalia's red sled; she's out there on it! Oh! Oh, why did we leave her? Now she'll be drowned, and it's all our fault!" Lynn slid down the rocky bank.

We were terribly frightened, and our cries, loud and hysterical, brought Mamma on the run.

"Thalia's overboard, Mamma, out by the kelp bed on her sled," we explained as we wept.

"Stop your noise and pray for her safety," Mamma answered. She closed her eyes and prayed: "God, keep her safe!"

Papa hurried past us, on his way to the boathouse. Mamma ran to the edge of the chasm. We followed, and stood watching the red sled as it bobbed in the current.

"Here, Curly—good dog. Fetch!" commanded Lynn. "Fetch!" Good old faithful Curly. He leaped into the sea and swam toward the sled.

The sled was bobbing and whirling with its precious burden; we hoped that Thalia wouldn't fall off into the churning water. We marveled that she was not screaming. She was silent, paralyzed with fear, no doubt.

Curly reached the sled and swam around it twice.

"Oh, I hope he knows enough to keep off the sled," worried Mamma.

"I hope he don't get tired and drown," I said, as Curly sank deep in the water. Curly found the rope, took it in his mouth, and began to tow the sled to shore.

Lynn called to him, "Fetch, boy; bring it here!" Curly reached the kelp bed, where the sled stuck fast in the kelp. The heroic dog sensed that he couldn't pull the sled through the mass of kelp. He crawled part way out of the water, and held the rope taut. The sled lay still against the kelp bed. At the moment, Papa brought the launch around the point, and hurried to the scene.

Curly gave a joyous bark when Papa lifted Thalia into the boat. "Good dog—good dog!" praised Papa, as he helped Curly out of the water. He rowed the launch to shore and handed the sled and Thalia to Lynn. "Her hands are frozen to the sled runners." Papa climbed out of the launch, then helped Curly out.

"Hold the line until I return. There's no place to tie up," he said to Lynn. He took the sled from Lynn and slowly made his way up the bank, where Mamma waited.

As he returned to the launch, we helped Mamma carry Thalia to the house. We watched while she worked to get Thalia's hands loose.

"How could her hands freeze in the hot sun?" I asked.

"Fear—not cold—has locked her hands," Mamma explained.

She heated a blanket over the stove and wrapped Thalia up.

"But, Mamma, it's so hot today!" protested René.

"She's suffering from shock," said Mamma. "She's very cold." She forced some brandy into Thalia's mouth.

When Papa and Curly came home, we rushed to the brave dog, petted and hugged him. Even Mamma, who didn't like to pet animals (because it made her hands smelly), petted Curly and called him brave.

Papa said, "If Curly hadn't pulled the sled to the kelp, it probably would have been too late when I got there. If we don't get off this god-damn island I'm afraid we'll lose some more children."

"'The thing which I greatly feared has come upon me,'" quoted Mamma.

"It won't be my fear that will bring us misfortune," flared Papa, "it will be your damned stubbornness."

"Curly ought to have a medal," declared Mamma. "He risked his life in those tide rips."

"Good old Curly," we praised him, again and again. When Thalia was out of danger, and sleeping, and the excitement of the horrible experience had quieted down a bit, Papa called us together for a conference.

"Today, you were given a charge to keep. I am ashamed of you, who failed in your trust. You deserted your baby sister on the dangerous grass slide. It is a miracle that she is alive. You would have had a very ugly memory to carry throughout your lives. You have proved yourselves untrustworthy, and I forbid any of you to use the grass slide again. In the first place, a grass slide anywhere on Patos is too dangerous and, in the second place, you must be punished for neglecting your duty. You must go into the woodshed and chop up your sleds, every one of them. And when you go to bed tonight, I want you to carry this thought with you: Duty is the first consideration of my life. Will you promise to do this?"

We did.

It was a saddened trio who filed to the woodshed to chop up the sleds. "Lynn," I asked, "do you like Thalia?"

"No," he answered, swinging the ax into our beautiful green sled, "not very much—but I wouldn't want her to drown."

Pre-1908 photo of Patos Island Lighthouse with third class Daboll Foghorn. Helene Glidden's father is the keeper on the left. *Photo courtesy of Coast Guard Museum Northwest*

CHAPTER FIVE

Of all the animals on Patos Island, I liked the pigs least—nasty, ill-tempered beasts that were always getting out of their pen and chasing us. I didn't like to feed them, because the pig food was so sloppy and so smelly.

We liked to feed the calves. Mamma warmed the milk, poured it into wooden buckets that we carried to the calfpens. There never were more than three calves in the pen at one time. Calves bunt so when drinking milk. They often bunted us over, pail and all.

One morning at breakfast, Papa announced that he had separated the latest calves from their mothers.

"I'm going to present you three children with these little heifers," he said. "They will be your very own. You'll have to teach them to drink all by yourselves, and when they are grown, you'll milk them yourselves." We were thrilled and a little awed. We had never taught a calf to drink.

"The milk's ready," called Mamma.

We scampered out. It didn't take long to reach the calfpen. There they stood—our own heifers.

"I choose the black-and-white," I said. "I'll name her Florabelle."

"Mine's Charm. She's the red one," Lynn shouted.

René had no choice but to accept the tiny white calf.

He named her Snowball.

It's a trick to teach a very young calf to drink, but we accomplished the feat with a maximum of bumps and bruises, and a minimum of spilled milk.

We took good care of our heifers. When they were old enough to leave the calfpen they followed us all over the island.

On Patos we picnicked a lot—on the beaches, in the woods, or across on Little Patos. Mamma knew just what to fix for a meal in the open—fresh baked bread, jam, fried chicken, pickled meats, baked beans with brown bread, cake, cold milk, and pickled fruits. Sometimes we walked to the picnic and sometimes we went in the boat. Once in a while, Al would take us to one of the other islands of the San Juan group.

We swam a lot, built sand huts, and hunted pretty shells or agates. Patos had some very unusual shells, and many agates. We kept our shell and agate collections in large glass jars on a shelf in the woodshed, along with our fish money. Whenever a pretty lady from Bellingham or Seattle visited us, Papa would give her any shell or agate she desired. Papa never could resist beautiful ladies. We soon learned to hide our choicest collections under the tank house.

We also collected wild birds' eggs; finches, hummingbirds, sparrows, wrens, thrushes, kingfishers, sea gulls, and sea pigeons. Mamma let us take only one egg out of each nest.

We hunted the large red sea urchins, some of which were as large as a man's head. The Indians who came to the island to gather seaweed taught us to open the sea egg and find a thick, yellow substance inside. This, they said, was good to eat. We tried it and found it very delicious. We rubbed the spines from the shell of the sea eggs, then allowed them to dry in the sun. After they were dry we polished them; the finished shell was added to our collection.

Another great sport was to gather the enormous kelp heads that grew all around the island. Papa used them for fertilizer. We used to cut faces in the largest of the heads, set them up and shoot at them. They were our enemies in many make-believe wars.

Trapping sea otters was a thrilling sport, and a profitable one. The skins sold at a good price. Mamma and the older girls all had otterskin coats.

When Lynn was ten, Papa gave him a small rifle. From then on we had a lot of fun hunting chicken hawks. Our chickens were so numerous that we didn't know how many we had. Many of the hens got out and nested in the woods. Sometimes we were able to catch the little chickens, but often we didn't, and were never surprised to run across a nest of eggs or a wild hen. Therefore the chicken hawks had a splendid hunting ground.

We shot owls and crows. Once I caught a crow that mangled one of my fingers before I could let it go. Some of the owls were ugly, too, especially the great snowy owl, about two feet high and with a wing spread of seven feet.

Sometimes one of them would swoop down at our heads when we played out of doors at night.

One of the greatest pleasures I remember was when the carpenters came to build the new lighthouse tower. We loved having the men live with us, because whenever we had guests our parents let up a little on our discipline. We especially liked Mr. Harris, the building engineer. He gave us the blocks of wood from the pieces the men sawed for the new building. Some of these blocks were very fancy. Mr. Harris was very kind to us children. He used to help us climb up the stair well to the tower. The stairway was not completed yet, so we climbed up a rope ladder. This was a thrilling experience because the ladder went winding around the stair well.

Patos light warned ships of the danger of Active Point, a long, treacherous spit that reaches out into 139 fathoms of water, said to be the swiftest and deepest in the San Juan Islands.

The outside of the tower had a guard rail all the way around it. We loved to stand out there, to watch the ships go by. Sometimes Papa let us use his binoculars; we took turns looking. Often, we could see people running about at East Point Lighthouse at Saturna, on the Canadian side of the channel. We could see rabbits hopping about on Skipjack, just as plain as if we were there.

The fog signal was an interesting place to us; we used to like to look through the door, while Papa and Al polished the brass of the equipment. Papa didn't allow any of us to go inside the fog signal or tower, except on the rare occasions when he took us, as a special treat. He was afraid we'd put fingerprints on the brass.

There were two large engines in the fog signal, standing side by side. To me, they looked forbidding, even when silent. When the engines were running, I could not be induced to go near the fog signal door. The noise frightened me to death, as did the booming foghorn.

The passing ships came in so close that we could hear the mumble of voices on them. These were the large ships of the Empress Line, sailing from Vancouver, B.C., to Australia. We loved the sound of the pounding engines, swishing waters, and "z-z-z-z-z," of the escaping steam. Night sounds over the water are eerie.

Before he went away, Mr. Harris built for us a large box swing. He hung it between the tall fir trees just outside the kitchen door. The swing was eight feet square, and was hung from a cross pole by two rods. In order to get into the swing, we had to climb a ladder. Once in, we propelled the huge box by pulling on a rope that was attached to a neighboring tree. The entire family could swing at one time.

Fishing was always a pleasant sport and often an adventure for us. Papa fished for halibut and salmon, but we were too small for anything that exciting, so we limited our fishing to cod. There were ling cod, kelp cod, and rock cod under the kelp beds and very near shore. Our custom was to row the boat to the kelp beds, put a kelp over the bow, thus anchoring her securely, and fish for hours at a time. We used meat for bait, but we didn't really need bait, the fish just bit on general principles. They just resented the fact that we threw our hooks into the water. Often I have seen a large ling cod come to the surface to bite at our toy boats.

Papa made us a live box, which we towed behind the boat. Whenever we had it full of fish, we sent them to Bellingham to be sold. The captain of the steamer *Elmo* handled our fish business for us. By prearrangement he always brought the money back in quarters, nickels, and dimes. Now, we three had never spent any money in our whole lives. We thought it was only something to be stored away in glass jars, like our shells and agates. Lynn was the oldest, so he took the quarters because they were the largest. I took the nickels, because they were next in size. René could have had the nickels, because he was older than I, but I had the stronger will, so he had to content himself with the little dimes. He was happy though, so my conscience didn't hurt much.

One day we were fishing in our accustomed place, when a boat suddenly appeared on the horizon. The sight of a boat was nothing unusual to us, but this one was coming toward the island. Not many boats came in so close.

"I wonder if she's coming here," said René.

"No," thought Lynn, "she's out too far in the straits, going to Blaine, I guess. Sure coming in fast; must have a good tide."

"Gosh," said René, "it sure is coming in too far. Maybe it's coming here after all."

For a short time we fished in silence, as we speculated on the large purse seiner, half hopeful that she was coming to the island.

Suddenly, she veered off her course and came in quite close.

"Crack! Crack!" A bullet hit our boat. "Crack!"

Others hit the water around us. Petrified, we waited, expecting to be hit at any moment.

Al, who had been watching the approach of the purse seiner, ran down the bank. "Lie down!" he ordered.

We all three dropped to the floor boards of the boat. The shots continued to fly. Al ran about on shore, shouting and waving his arms.

Papa, who witnessed the scene from the tower, ran quickly down to the engine room and sounded the foghorn. Al, fearing that because we were silent we must have been hit by the flying shots, hurried to the flag stand and raised the flag upside down.

Contrary to custom, the large purse seiner did not come in. She majestically swung out into the straits and proceeded on her way. Papa rushed to the tower and, grabbing his field glasses, ascertained her name, *Petrel*. Then, running along the shore, he joined Al, and both called to us.

"René, answer me!" commanded Al.

Silence reigned in the lifeboat. Lynn was frightened dumb. René and I were white and speechless. We all lay prone, gazing at five large holes in the lifeboat.

Al leaped into the water and swam frantically out to the lifeboat. Grasping the gunwale, he pulled himself up, afraid of what he might see.

When I saw the hand and leg come over the side of the boat, my vocal cords were released and I began to scream lustily. This broke the tension, and Lynn and René both sat up.

"Why didn't you answer me?" questioned Al. "I couldn't," said Lynn. "I thought I was dead." Late that afternoon, a ship, passing by, responded to the forgotten upside-down flag. Al went to Bellingham with the captain, to search out the sharpshooters and bring them to justice. When apprehended, the men professed no memory of seeing a distress signal. In court, the procedure was almost comical.

Judge: "Clifton Bruce, you were employed on the *Petrel* in July?"

Bruce: "Yes, your Honor."

Judge: "You remember shooting at three children in a lifeboat?"

Bruce: "No, your Honor. We did shoot at three sea gulls on a log, near Patos Island, but as soon as we killed them, we quit."

Judge: "Were you aware that shooting sea gulls is illegal?"

Bruce: "No, your Honor. I'm a college student, employed for the summer only. I know nothing about maritime law."

Judge: "Did you hear five blasts of a foghorn?"

Bruce: "Yes, but we thought the keeper was testing his equipment."

Judge: "Did you see the flag of the United States flying upside down?"

Bruce: "No, your Honor; there was no breeze. We noticed the flag, but we couldn't see it very well."

Judge: "Do you know what it means when the flag is reversed?"

Bruce: "No, your Honor."

Judge: "Mr. Clark [Al], do you think these men knew that they were shooting at children or persons in a boat?"

Al: "I'm not sure what they knew, but they were in very close— I could see them plainly."

Judge: "What did you do after you made the children lie down?"

Al: "I ran the flag up. It was flying in a good breeze—unmistakable to any mariner."

Judge: "Lynn, do you think these men were shooting at you?"

Lynn: "Yes, sir, they shot at us and made five holes in our U.S.L.H.E. boat."

Judge: "Angela, what do you think happened while you were fishing?"

Angie: "A boat came in close, and bang-bang, someone shot at us. They really shot me, but I didn't die, cause they didn't shoot me dead."

Judge: "We continue this case later. I see no need for the children to remain. It is a pure case of ignorance of the maritime law, and will be tried in a suitable court."

For a long time we were frightened whenever a boat passed us as we fished from our lifeboat.

Mamma was complaining of something or someone raiding her henhouse. She wasn't getting as many eggs as she thought she should. The henhouse was quite a distance from our house, and secluded by a grove of trees. Of course, Mamma accused me, and for good reason too. I liked to suck eggs. It was a habit of mine to punch a hole in an egg, and after blowing out the white, to suck out the yolk. But I only took the eggs that I found outside the chickenyard. I believed them to be rightfully mine because I had hunted out the hidden nests.

Yet I was wrongly punished on several occasions for this offense, and I became resentful. "How do you know that I take your eggs, Mamma?"

"Because God tells me so," she answered. "He knows everything you do."

I thought this very unfair of God. Especially since tattling was one of the sins strictly forbidden.

One early morning, before daylight, I determined to find out who really took the eggs. Accompanied by Curly, I went to the henhouse and got up on the shelf over the door. I was almost asleep when all of a sudden the door was pushed open, and someone entered. In the gray light I recognized the bearded and bewhiskered face of the man I had seen in the woods! I was completely surprised to see Curly wag his tail in welcome. The intruder reached down and scratched Curly's ears. "Good boy," he said.

I held my breath in fear. Then with righteous indignation I shouted. "Get out of here, you old God—you old tattletale God! So, you steal the eggs and then you tell Mamma that I do. You old God-thief!" He looked exactly like the picture in the front of the Bible. I had no doubt that it was really God, and I didn't think much of him.

Very suddenly he ran out of the henhouse, and when I told Mamma she punished me again.

After this unwarranted punishment, I determined to keep it a secret if I should ever see God on the island again. Mamma was so unbelieving. All I had said was "Mamma, I saw God in the henhouse, and he was stealing your eggs, and I called him a thief."

"You're fast becoming a little liar," she said, and promptly washed out my mouth with her nasty homemade soap.

Word got around, and soon the rest of the family began to make fun of me. It wasn't long before I began to wonder what was different about me.

"Didn't I really see the old man?" I asked myself. I was still very young, and this thing worried me. I began to take long walks alone, to escape the family's joking. On these walks I often caught glimpses of the bearded face in the woods. I wondered why the others didn't see it, too, but I was silent on the subject.

It was about this time that I began to hear voices. Voices that told me to do or not to do things. I remembered the first day that I saw Patos, and how I had been so sure that the island had smiled.

"Perhaps she did smile on that day, and now in my aloneness, the island is talking to me." I kept these thoughts to myself as much as possible, but the fact that I heard voices leaked out, and then Mamma added another word that the others took up and tormented me with.

"You are either a very good liar, or are psychic," she said. The others took up this word to torment me with.

"Angie's psychic, Angie's psychic!" they shouted. From then on I walked very much alone. I didn't know what psychic meant, but I fancied that it was pretty terrible, and that Mamma must hate me to call me such a name.

I had just finished reading a story about a little boy who didn't have a father. Every night the boy lighted a candle on his prie-dieu, and prayed to a saint to bring him a father. His prayers were finally answered, and the boy lived happily ever after.

I thought I'd like to pray to a saint, only I didn't have a prie-dieu, and I didn't know what a saint was. I thought, "How nice it would be if I prayed to a saint asking him to make Mamma believe me about seeing God—and he'd answer my prayers."

One day I asked Al, "What is a prie-dieu, and what is a saint?"

He carefully told me about the Catholics and their way of worship. It sounded grand to me.

"I'd like to pray to a saint," I said. "I'd like to light candles. Do you know a good saint to pray to?"

Al hesitated a moment before saying, "I guess the only saint I know is St. Nicholas. Perhaps he'd do. As long as it's only an experiment, I guess no harm will come of it."

I found a large picture of St. Nicholas in Mamma's Christmas things, also some pretty red candles. After searching the island carefully for a secluded spot that would be quite safe from the prying eyes of my brothers and sisters, I found a cave in a hollow tree. The tree was on the top of a cliff overlooking the sound, not too far from home.

I nailed the bright picture of St. Nicholas to the wall of the cave. Next I placed an old milk stool under it in lieu of a prayer bench. Then I put the candles in two fruit jars, so the flames wouldn't set fire to the tree cave. I set them firmly in wax so they'd stand up.

I stood back viewing my work. It was a most beautiful prie-dieu. I knelt on the milk stool and prayed, "Please, St. Nicholas, ask God to make the kids like me, and make Mamma believe that I saw God. And don't tell God I asked you to do this. Amen."

My prayers were answered. The next day everyone treated me very graciously. Overjoyed, I took Estelle into my confidence and showed her my prie-dieu.

"Oh, no!" she exclaimed. "Angel, you mustn't. It says in the Ten Commandments, 'Thou shalt have no other gods before me. Thou shalt not bow down thyself to them nor serve them—for I the Lord thy God am a jealous God—'"

"*Well,*" I answered, "I don't care. He has no business being jealous. Besides, St. Nicholas answered my prayers, and I'll go on praying to him. You won't tell Mamma, will you?"

"No," Estelle answered, "but please don't pray too much. I'm afraid."

"I'll be careful, and only pray when I have to," I promised.

But I didn't keep my promise. I visited the prie-dieu on every little occasion when I was disturbed in spirit. I prayed for everything and about everything. It was easy to pray to beautiful St. Nicholas, because I knew him. And I was proud of my beautiful prie-dieu.

"I'll pray to you, too, sometimes, God—just so you won't get jealous," I promised.

"Well, I am jealous. Take down that picture of Santa Claus!" It was the same voice that I had heard before, telling me to do things.

I sat, too stunned to run away.

"Take it down!' The voice thundered again.

I looked up at the hole above my head, and there was God!

"God!" I gulped and drew back against the wall of the cave, my hand hastily ripping the St. Nicholas picture from its place.

"Now, in the future, pray to God alone, and not to foolish idols. I've been watching you from this hole for several days."

"All right, God—all right—" I stammered. "Are you the voice I hear all the time when I'm alone in the woods?"

"That may be," he answered. "Now I command you to stop telling people about me. If you tell anyone, I'll leave Patos Island—never to return. How would you like to live on Patos without a God?"

"Oh, I wouldn't want you to leave," I answered. "I won't tell about you, and I'll bring bread and things for you to eat. Please don't go away!" Then I asked, "Why don't you want people to know you live here, instead of Heaven?"

"Because some people don't want God to live on earth. Your papa would turn me in to the Coast Guard, for living on Patos. It's a private island."

"I won't tell on you. Please stay on Patos. I love you, God. I love you very much!"

I ran outside and around the tree. There was no one there. I crept back inside my prayer tree.

"God, God," I prayed. "Please come back, and I'll bring you eggs so you won't have to steal 'em any more. God, I'll bring the things to my tree and you can find 'em here whenever you want 'em."

Then I heard a voice that seemed to come from the roots of the tree. "I'll be here whenever you pray. Don't forget to pray to God alone."

I shivered violently, and jumping up, ran all the way home. I desperately wanted to tell someone of my experience, but God had made me promise not to tell.

That night I heard Mamma say to Papa, "I declare, that Angie is getting queerer all the time. Estelle says she prays in a tree—and of all things, to St. Nicholas."

"Let her pray," said Papa. "I used to pray to a wooden doll when I was young. Kids like to see what they're praying to, and you can't see God."

But you could. I wanted to tell him that God was really alive and on Patos, but I didn't dare.

New Dungeness Lighthouse where Helene Glidden was born in 1900. The original 100-foot tower, as it appears in this photo, was constructed in 1857 and shortened to 63 feet in 1927. *Photo courtesy of Coast Guard Museum Northwest*

CHAPTER SIX

One of our greatest pleasures was visiting on the Coast Guard cutter that frequently anchored in the bay. It wasn't always the same cutter; sometimes it was the *Guard* and sometimes the *Arcata*. We enjoyed talking to the crew of the two boats. When we asked them why they lay in the bay at Patos, they laughed and said, "Now that would be telling," or "Perhaps we stand guard here to watch you kids so you'll behave yourselves and mind your parents." But a fisherman told Lynn that the Coast Guard was hiding in the bay because they were on the lookout for smugglers and hijackers.

"There aren't any smugglers and hijackers on Patos," I said.

"No, but they have come here before, and they might return," said René. "I heard that Spanish John was last seen near here. He might come to Patos to hide. He is the leader of the opium ring that Papa nearly broke up when we lived in Port Townsend. I wish he'd come here so Papa could catch him."

"Well, I don't," I answered, "and Mamma don't either. She wants to stay on Patos Island until we're grown up, and if Papa catches Spanish John we'll have to go back to town."

"I wonder who's going to win—Papa or Mamma,"

Lynn squinted his eyes and looked out over the water.

"How do you mean 'win'?" I asked.

"Oh, they're always quarreling about whether we stay on Patos or go to town. I hope Mamma wins. I like to live here."

"I want to stay here too," I said.

"Then you'd better quit talking silly about seeing God and hearing voices, because I heard Papa and Mamma talking, and they intend to send you away to a funny school for silly people. Mamma says you have a twisted mind."

"I'm not twisted!" I yelled. "I really talk to God!"

"Oh, you don't either. I know who you talk to, but I know enough to keep my mouth shut. You don't catch me going around babbling about seeing God."

"Do you see him too, Lynn? Do you?" I asked.

"You don't get me to say nothing. You're not goin' to get me to tell anything so they'll all call me crazy and queer. No, siree, I keep my mouth shut. And you'd better too, or you'll be sent away."

"I won't say anything either, from now on," I promised. I meant to keep my promise, but it was too hard; I often broke it.

An important-looking letter came in the morning mail. Mamma read it to Papa. It was from Colonel Roosevelt, telling Papa that the U.S. fleet was going to pass Patos.

Mamma read the letter again, so Papa would have it right. He wanted to be sure of the day.

Dear Ed:

On June 20, the fleet will pass your lighthouse. Don't fail to be on hand to receive the official salute from "Binny," our mutual friend. I have instructed him to dip three times; once for me, once for himself, and once for auld lang syne.

I think of you often and, someday when I am free of my responsibility, I'll be out there to catch one of those big *tyees* you're always bragging about.

I'll be thinking of you, as the fleet goes by.

As ever, your friend,
Theodore Roosevelt.

Papa laughed happily. "Well, I'll be god-damned," he said. He took the letter in his own hands and scanned it, as if he could read what was written there. "Well, the old son of a gun," he laughed. "A special salute for me. Well, Binny, my boy, I'll have a special salute for you, too." Chuckling, he tucked the letter in his pocket.

Papa always carried Teddy Roosevelt's letters around for days. He and Mr. Roosevelt had been best friends many years ago, when they were very young.

I didn't know who the Binny referred to in the letter was. Later I found that he was the cook on the flagship.

On the scheduled day for the appearance of the fleet, we were up early; we could scarcely contain ourselves, we were so excited.

"Sixteen battleships! Gee!" said Lynn. We hadn't seen *any* battle-ships before. We couldn't eat our breakfast.

"Let's go down to the fog signal and watch for them," I said. We went out, and down the walk to the lighthouse. Climbing onto a high rock, we sat and scanned the horizon for a glimpse of smoke. In about an hour, we were rewarded with the sight of a gray hulk.

"Run and tell Papa," shrieked Lynn. He didn't want to miss any part of the approach, himself. I ran to the house.

"They're coming! They're coming!" I yelled.

Everyone ran out. "Come on," shouted Papa, "you can all stand in the tower." We ran quickly, and in a few moments had climbed the stairs to the tower. Papa stayed in the engine room; he wanted to blow the horn, in salute, as the flagship went by. Al manned the flagpole, to be ready to dip the flag. Mamma took charge of the small children in the tower, so no small fingers should smudge the brass or glass lenses.

We watched the giant ships approach. We could see the waves part, as the sharp bows cut through the water. It was a glorious sight.

Soon the flagship was passing the point. "Bow-w-w!" roared the horn.

"Boo-o-o!" answered the ship. I glanced at the flagpole. Al loos-ened the rope, dipped the flag once, twice, three times. In answer, the flag on the flagship dipped three times—one for the Colonel, one for Binny, and one for auld lang syne. Papa hurried to the tower, raised his cap, and waved it again and again.

"Boo-oo-o," said the flagship, in passing. The other ships glided by: the *Delaware, Tennessee, Arkansas, New Mexico, Colorado,* and all the rest—sixteen of them.

We waved our hands, jumped up and down, and shouted, "Good-bye! Good-bye!" We waved until the last ship was far past the island. Then, with happy hearts, we slowly went down from the tower.

"Gee," said Lynn. "Sixteen battleships!"

It was nearing the end of our second summer. Everyone was in a high state of excitement. Mamma had decided that Roy, Clara, and Estelle should go to Bellingham to school.

The sewing machine had been rattling for days as Mamma and Mary sewed. Roy had seven new shirts, and the girls had guimpes, jumpers, petticoats, and panties all shining with newness and decorating every chair back. Papa said that the place resembled a laundry.

Papa went to Bellingham and arranged boarding accommodations for the three young people. Estelle was to live with Dr. Larkin, Roy with the Harveys, and Clara with Captain Chase, captain of the steamer *Elmo.*

The day arrived. The three boarded the *Elmo* and, with never a backward look at the tearful group on the shore, set out for new adventure.

The Christmas holidays arrived, bringing Roy, Clara, and Estelle home for two weeks. We were glad to see them. They had changed a lot. Clara and Estelle talked a great deal of boys and dancing parties. Estelle had several new recitations that she gave at our Christmas Eve party. Mamma thought that her technique had greatly improved.

Clara had learned some new songs and sang them, much to our delight. We especially liked "Smarty, Smarty, Smarty," "Not Because Your Hair Is Curly," and "Two Little Girls in Blue."

Roy limped slightly. Mamma asked him what caused the limp, and he told her of a bicycle accident. He had been learning to ride a friend's bicycle, had lost control, plunged down a steep hill, and landed in a briar patch, bumping his knee against a boulder. Mamma looked worried. She rolled up his trouser leg and examined the knee. It looked all right but it was painful to the touch. Mamma applied arnica and wrapped the knee in a flannel cloth.

Roy still limped when he left for Bellingham, a week later.

The first rays of the rising sun warmed the early morning air; the sunbeams danced on the pools of sea water, lending enchantment to the scene. Estelle carried a basket on her arm. From time to time Lynn, René and I would run back to put some newly found curio into it. One of Estelle's teachers had expressed a desire to own a marine-life collection; Estelle was bent on fulfilling it.

"Oh, come here! Come here!" squealed René, as he leaned over a deep-water pool. We hurried to see what he had found.

"It's a basket fish," exclaimed Estelle. "A beauty."

We peered down through the clear water, to see a curious object lying on the white sand at the bottom of the pool.

"It is a basket fish!" excitedly agreed Lynn. "Let's get it out."

"How can we get it?" asked Estelle. "The pool is so deep, and too narrow for diving."

"We'll get a forked pole," Lynn decided, "and lift him out."

The boys found a branch, which, when whittled down, suited their purpose. Lynn reached to lift the basket fish out of its bed. Estelle lay on the rocks and stretched her body out over the pool, with outstretched arms, ready to catch the fish as Lynn brought it to the surface. Gently, Lynn forced the basket fish to the top of the water. Estelle caught it and dropped it into the basket. It was a curious-looking object, somewhat like a starfish, but with tapering, lacelike legs—fourteen of them. We had several basket fish at home. Papa had cured them by dropping them into lye-water to kill the animal, rinsed them of the lye-water, shaped them like a basket, and hung them to dry in the sun. The baskets were very beautiful, lacelike affairs.

We walked far out on the reef. Lying on our stomachs, we watched the animal movement in the beautiful, underwater garden. There were anemones of all colors, purple, pink, green, and particolored; purple sea plumes and brightly colored fans; jellyfish, trailing long streamers as they throbbed, in passing. There were barnacles and coral, all covered with tube worms, which burst into pastel flowers as we watched, conch shells and gray shrimp. Sometimes we saw the giant, wavy-shelled clams, with many-colored mantles. We were never able to catch one of these clams, and Papa said it was a good thing we didn't because they were very vicious.

Tiring of our positions on the barnacled rocks, we continued on our way, searching everywhere for objects of interest for Estelle's basket.

We climbed high on the rocks, to hunt in the crevices for the nests of sea pigeons. Gathering an egg from each of several nests, we soon had enough to make a fine collection.

"I'd like to get a sea gull's egg," remarked Estelle.

Lynn became thoughtful. "I know where there is a nest," he said, "but Papa warned us to keep away; the gulls get mean when they're nesting."

"If we all go up, perhaps we can frighten her away from the nest long enough to grab an egg," urged Estelle.

"I'm not going," announced René.

"*I'm* not afraid," I answered.

We walked around the point, stopped a moment to pet our heifers, which were grazing with the herd on a grassy slope. A short distance on, we came to the cliff, where stood an old, bleached, dead tree. In the high branches was an eagle's nest.

"The sea gull's nest is in that cliff," said Lynn, "near the roots of the eagle's tree."

Estelle set her basket down in a safe place, and began to climb the rocks.

"Missus sea gull, here I come," she called.

I followed her.

Lynn picked up a stick. "Just in case," he said, and followed us up the slope. It was a difficult ascent. The foot places were narrow and often crumbled under our weight, forcing us to grab quickly at anything that afforded us an anchor.

We had almost reached the sea gull's nest, when suddenly we were frozen to our positions by a bloodcurdling scream. Almost immediately, the great bald eagle swooped down upon Estelle. She lost her footing and hung, clinging to a crevice. I, the unafraid, went sliding, bumping, and falling to the rocks beneath.

Lynn struck again and again at the fierce bird, as he sank his talons into Estelle's shoulders. Her blouse was ripped away, and blood oozed from two long scratches. Estelle made not a sound. At the first attack of the eagle, René fainted dead away. Lynn's blows managed to break one of the eagle's legs, and to damage a wing. The great bird fluttered to a crag, and rested, screaming like one insane.

Lynn caught Estelle. "Hurry down," he said. "His mate will be along any minute."

Estelle couldn't move. Lynn tore her hands loose from the rocks. He dragged her down the rough cliffside, tearing her clothes and skinning her arms and legs. From a torn place near her shoulder blade, a stream of blood oozed.

Estelle finally returned to her senses. "We've got to stop the bleeding," she said weakly. "Angel, give me your white panties; mine are black sateen, and the dye might infect the wound." I took off my underthings and handed them over.

"Now run, Angie," commanded Lynn. "Tell Papa to bring the boat around."

I ran. Climbing the bluff, I passed the herd again. A bright idea entered my mind. Turning back, I sought out the black calf, which we often rode. Flinging my legs over his back, I settled down, and grabbed his tail.

"Giddap," I ordered, turning his head toward home. The black calf fairly bolted over the ground. I bounced up and down on his back, and was very uncomfortable in my pantless skin.

At the barnyard gate, I dismounted. Crawling under the fence, I ran wildly to the house, announcing in a screeching tone, "The bald eagle dug a hole in Estelle! Get out the boat to bring her carcass home!"

Papa hurried to the boathouse.

Mamma quieted me down a little and then asked, "Is Estelle dead?"

"No," I answered, "she's not dead. She's got a hole in her, though, and my panties are in the hole." I pulled up my dress and let Mamma see the sore places where the calf's rough hair had rubbed the skin from my unprotected seat.

After a long while, Papa brought Estelle in. She was very ill and white from shock and loss of blood. There was a nasty tear in her back. Mamma worked over it a long time, disinfecting and sewing up the edges.

René carried the basket of sea pigeons' eggs into the kitchen.

"I don't think I want those eggs," said Estelle. "I don't think I'll ever rob sea gulls' nests again, or sea pigeons'."

At East Sound, the next morning, when Papa had taken Estelle to a doctor, he bought Lynn a beautiful hunting knife. "Just in case," said Papa.

"Come on, Angie," called Lynn. "The tide's in. Let's go to the boathouse and play with our little boats."

I put down my doll, and ran after him. It was always a pleasure to go to the boathouse. Here was where we kept our fleet of tiny boats. Many of them were homemade, but we had some beauties that were hand carved by the Kanaka Bay Indians. These were works of art. There was one especially interesting even to the grown-ups who visited the island. It was a large canoe carved from birchwood. It had a full set of hand-carved warriors seated in it, in the regular order of rank. Some of the warriors had fancy headdresses, others were bareheaded, but they all had real Indian hair, long and flowing. We had launches, rowboats, battleships, barges, and tugs, all exquisitely carved.

We liked to pretend that the boats were real. We made a raft of miniature logs, to be towed by the tugs, had real battles with the battleships, made little people out of empty spools for passengers and crews of all the boats. We had piers, harbors, and sometimes, when the tide was in far enough, we dug rivers in the sand, floating our boats up the river. We had pirate fights, capsizing the boats and capturing each other's men. There was no end to the pleasure afforded by our boats.

Today we decided to tow logs. We agreed to have a storm, and wreck the rafts and have fun rounding up the logs and putting them back into the booms. Lynn got a paddle and began to make rough water. I held the tug and boom, towing it into the storm, when suddenly the string broke. Before I could grab it, the tugboat drifted into deep water and began to be sucked in by the strong tide of the bay. We were very fond of that little red tug. We hated to lose it. But it was too far out to be reached with poles, and we could do nothing but watch.

"Maybe it will drift in when the tide changes," I consoled.

"No, it won't," said Lynn. "It's heading for the channel."

After a few moments of hopeless watching, we gathered up the remaining boats and carried them into the boathouse. We both looked at the lifeboat, resting on the car.

"I wish we could let it down," said Lynn. "We could each take an oar and row out after the tug."

"Let's do it!" I suggested. "We can tie her to the car with a long rope, and when the car goes under water she will float clear. Then I can pull her in by the rope."

This sounded reasonable to Lynn, so he agreed. He would knock out the prop that held the cable in place. I would sit in the boat. This plan would have worked too, if only we had remembered to tie the painter to the car.

Lynn knocked out the prop, the car rolled rapidly down the track, unbalancing me as I stood in the descending boat, and losing one oar as it struck water. It shot out into the current of the bay with me in it. I tried to manage the long, heavy oar, but the current was too much for me. The big lifeboat was swept into the tide rips.

In just a few moments I was being pulled toward the awful whirlpools that abound off the point of Little Patos. As the boat was seized and started to whirl, I began to scream. I had always wished that I might look down into one of these whirlpools. I did, and those of you who have never looked down into a whirlpool can thank your lucky stars that you have been spared this horror.

In a very short time I was nauseated. I fell into the bottom of the boat and began to vomit. I didn't care whether I survived or not.

The danger of my predicament then dawned on me. There was no other boat at Patos Island. Al being away with the launch, I was entirely without hope of rescue.

After an eternity the whirlpool spent itself, and the boat was set free. I climbed back to the seat, only to see my island receding in the distance. On the shore, tiny specks ran about waving to me. I noticed that the flag was flying and was upside down. The fog signal was bawling loud and long. There wasn't a ship in sight, and Papa's efforts at rescue were all in vain.

Night came on. I lay down in the bottom, weeping. During that first long night I thought of all the naughty things I had done. I wept and prayed. I forgave God for tattling on me. I began to promise him all sorts of things if he'd get me out of my predicament.

"Oh, God," I prayed, "I don't know how to pray pretty like Al does, but if you get me out of this I'll let you have all the eggs you want." I waited. Nothing happened, so I began again.

"God," I said, 'I'll even cook some of the eggs for you." I waited a moment for this last promise to sink in, and then when I saw I wasn't getting anywhere with God, I shouted. "God! Didn't you hear me? I'll bring you a loaf of Mamma's fresh bread. God—I'll leave the bin open so you can get bran—" I realized I wasn't getting any place, so I determined to go all the way in my promises. "God," I said, "I'll get you some of Mamma's brown sugar lumps. I'll steal them out of the pantry for you, God."

Then I knew with a feeling of hopeless sickness that God wasn't paying the slightest attention to me. I became angry. "Damn old God, I hate you! You old God; you old damn God!"

Hours later, I repented. "I'm sorry, God," I said. "I didn't mean it, but I'm so cold and so sick. Please help me. I'll give you my teddy bear." I had nothing more to offer. My teddy bear was my dearest possession.

A school of blackfish appeared and began to spout very near the boat. I remembered the tales I had heard about the blackfish upsetting fishing boats near the island. I remembered what Al told me about the Twenty-third Psalm. I began to repeat it: "Yea, though I walk through the valley of the shadow ... I will fear no evil." A blackfish spouted too close. "Oh, God," I screamed, "I *am* afraid! I *am* afraid!"

Two days later, I was returned to consciousness by the sound of voices, and a grappling hook striking against the side of the boat. I recognized the cutter *Arcata*. I was lifted aboard and wrapped in a blanket. The skipper tried to force something between my swollen, bleeding lips. I was too sick to care what happened to me now. I closed my eyes.

In a few hours I could talk a little, and the first thing I said was "Did God send you?"

"Yes," answered the skipper. "He told me you were out here."

"I prayed," I said.

Late that afternoon I was returned home, but for a long time I lay in bed, sometimes delirious, sometimes just too tired to move. Mamma fed me tons of quinine, which was punishment enough for meddling with the boat.

Patos Island Lighthouse with tower added in 1908. The lighthouse was originally operated by the United States Lighthouse Establishment (U.S.L.H.E.).
Photo courtesy of Coast Guard Museum Northwest

CHAPTER SEVEN

66 "Red sky at morning, sailors take warning;
"Red sky at night, sailors delight." Mamma chanted this
as she looked out the window. I glanced out the window
too—the sky in the east was a brilliant red.

Immediately the cold wind swooped in from the northwest,
cutting like icy knives through our clothing, chilling us to the bone.
It was impossible to walk from the house to the fog signal. Papa
crawled the distance on his hands and knees to prevent being blown
overboard. Two of our wooden washtubs had been left outside that
morning. We watched them as they rolled before the wind and
splashed into the sea.

Mary and Mamma worked frantically to bring in the washing,
which Mamma had hung out to dry only an hour before. With a
deafening roar, the icy giant wrenched the clothes, line and all, from
the startled women's hands. The sheets were converted into sails. As
the washing sped through the air we shouted in hilarious laughter
to see Papa's long union suit, filled with wind, go ballooning over
the sea—to land like a snow-white corpse on a giant wave. Curly
wanted to retrieve the washing. Mamma had to tie him up to prevent
him from pursuing it.

All day the wind roared about the great house, lashing it with
gray sea spume filled with sand, which became embedded in the
white paint.

"We'll have to paint the whole damned house over when this is
done," said Papa.

Night came. Still the wind howled, rattling the storm shutters. It prevented us from sleeping. Around midnight, Papa wakened Mamma.

"Get up," he said, "and make some black coffee. There's a boat in distress on our west side." Papa then awakened Al. I could hear their muffled voices through the walls.

When Mamma went downstairs, I hastily got out of bed and dressed. From the window I could see the dark hulk of a boat, being swept by the wind toward the dangerous rocky reefs. Someone on the boat was signaling with a lantern. Papa circled his lantern above his head, in answer.

I ran down to the rocks where Papa and Al were. The wind was less violent now. There was at least no danger of being blown overboard, though we had to brace ourselves against the awful wind. Al had brought pike poles, grappling hooks, and lines from the boathouse. The two men set their lanterns down, and stood waiting for the helpless boat.

"She's going to hit the reef," said Al.

"God! I hope you're wrong," said Papa.

They walked toward the reef, carrying the pike poles, grappling hooks, and lines. Papa noticed me.

"Bring the lanterns," he ordered.

I picked up both lanterns and followed.

"If she strikes the reef, we can't save her," said Papa. "No one can live in this hellish storm."

It had begun to rain now. I pulled my jacket up over my head. The cold rain hissed as it struck the hot glass of the lanterns.

"Maybe we can reach her before she hits," said Al. They walked far out on the slippery rocks.

The boat drew near. It was a large fishing sloop. The wind and waves were driving her relentlessly toward the reef. She was almost upon the rocks now. Papa and Al lunged out with the pike poles. They missed, lunged again, and struck the wood of the sloop's side.

"Hallo-o-o," shouted Papa.

"Hallo-o-o," a voice from the boat answered.

"Heave your l-i-i-ne," Papa shouted again. The wind was against him; his voice couldn't be understood by the sloop's owner. Papa and Al pulled in their pike poles and lunged again at the hulk. Driving the sharp irons into the wood, the two men began to push the tossing boat off the rocks and back along the shore of the island.

"Give us a line," shouted Papa. The man aboard understood.

"No line," he shouted back.

"Hold her," said Al. "I'll tie a rock to a line and toss it to him." He quickly fastened a rock to one end of a line and tossed it to the sloop. "It's so dark I can't see where it's going," he shouted.

The rock found its mark. The boat's owner picked up the line and secured it to his snubbing post. Al pulled the rope taut, and began to walk away from the reef. He snubbed the line, first on one rock and then on another, as he progressed. Papa pushed from behind with the pike pole. The lurching hulk slowly moved up the island toward the deep-water shoreline.

"It's a damned big boat for a crew of one," said Papa.

It was daylight before the men had pulled and pushed the sloop to safety, but not before she was badly damaged by the pounding she had taken on the rocks. The giant waves still lashed her. It was with difficulty that her owner was helped ashore by Al, while Papa held the hulk with a grappling hook.

The man stood very near me on the shore. He was black visaged, dirty, and *smelled*. I was soaking wet from the rain and cold and, when the odor of the man reached my nostrils, I began to vomit. No one noticed me.

"Where you from?" asked Papa.

The dirty man spoke brokenly. "Me, I Tom—Indian Tom—they call me. You very thinky to save me, Cap'n—very thinky for sure. I come with message. Blanchard very sick in Bellin'ham. Want you come—on'y my boat—she so bad hurt—you haf' wait for steamer come. Mebbe Blanchard he die meanwhile."

Mr. Blanchard always wintered in Bellingham. We hadn't seen

him for several months. Papa was impressed with the message Indian Tom brought.

"Hell-on-earth! Did you brave this storm to bring me that message?" roared Papa. "Man, you're a fool!"

"Blanchard—he mebbe die," said the Indian. "He got 'portant message. You mebbe need to know."

In Mamma's brightly polished kitchen, Indian Tom was very much out of place. He smelled horribly. His wet clothes hung dirty and ragged; his unwashed face was scaly with dirt. His unkempt hair was black and oily.

Mamma gingerly served him with hot coffee, followed by a breakfast of bacon, eggs, and toast. Then she motioned Papa into the hallway.

"What are we going to do with him?" she asked.

Papa didn't know. "His boat is badly damaged. We'll have to keep him until we can repair it."

"Well," blazed Mamma, "I'm sure of one thing. That human compost pile won't get between my white sheets."

"I'll go to East Sound and take the boat to Bellingham," Papa said to Mamma.

"Oh, no, you don't," said Mamma. "Not until this shipwreck is out of the way. I'll not be responsible for this smelly bundle of woe."

When he had eaten, Indian Tom accompanied Papa while he milked the cows. Mary entered the kitchen. "Phew," she said, "where's the dead fish?"

Mamma began to cry. "Oh, whatever shall we do? We can't keep him here."

Indian Tom was for sure quite a problem. Papa fixed him a bed in the tool shed, immediately adjoining the barn. "Because," he explained, "this is government property, and we're not allowed to keep strangers on the premises."

Indian Tom took him at his word, and didn't seem offended.

Early next morning, when I poked my head inside the barn door, the cows looked positively nauseated. Indian Tom came to the house for his meals, however, and no one felt very hungry when he was near.

For two days we entertained our "soiled problem." Then Papa and Al towed the foul-smelling sloop to the Head-of-the-Bay and beached it. They propped the old black boat up, and Indian Tom went back to his own housekeeping.

"We'll have to fumigate," Mamma said.

When the *Elmo* came, Papa went to Bellingham to see Mr. Blanchard. We were impatient for his return. We were very fond of Mr. Blanchard. It worried us to know that he was gravely ill.

When Papa returned we were desolated by his tidings.

"He didn't live long enough to give me the message," he said. "He mumbled something about Spanish John. I caught the word 'hiding'—and something about an old rocker. I don't know what he wanted to tell me."

"I guess he meant to tell you to keep his belongings," said Mamma. "He often told me to help myself to his books if he should pass away during the winter months. He has some valuable histories of the San Juans in his cabin."

"He probably knew where Spanish John is hiding," said Papa. "It's just my luck to miss his last words."

Papa and Mamma carried Mr. Blanchard's books from the cabin to our house. Al boarded up the old cabin. In a short time the weeds grew so densely around it that it was almost forgotten by the family.

Repairing Indian Tom's old black boat took longer than Papa had anticipated, and for three weeks it lay on the Head-of-the-Bay beach, its odor rendering the air so nauseating that we were unable to approach the beach. Indian Tom was a ratfish fisherman. The oil from the ratfish sold in San Francisco for very high prices.

"It's a good business," Papa declared, "but a stinking one. I hope he never gets shipwrecked on Patos again!"

Though Mr. Blanchard was gone, one of the Patos harbors continued to be called Blanchard's Harbor and is so called to this day. Here the biggest San Juan group of seals were accustomed to gather in our day, and still do. Early each morning we could hear them mooing and barking. It was fun to walk to a point opposite the seal rock, yell and scream and watch them go padding into the water, the mothers pushing and slapping their babies to hurry them. We didn't do this very often, though, because Papa always punished us for making unnecessary noises.

These were the gray seals. They had beautiful silvery gray coats, spotted with black and brown patches.

The cow seals always calved in March of each year. In May, when the water was calm enough, Papa let us take the boat around the island.

As we approached the seal rock, the seals scrambled into the water to come snooping up to investigate us from the shelter of deep water.

We always sat very still, so the baby seals would come near the boat.

On one particular morning we made the trip to the seal rock. When the seals became accustomed to the presence of our boat, they came up all around us, some even braving the danger to climb to the rock again.

We began a slow, mournful, cooing whistle in a low key. It wasn't long before the young seals approached the boat to investigate. After a long time, we slowly extended our hands. Some of the calves immediately sank, but we were rewarded for our patience. René and I each touched a shiny head. We moved our fingers across the skull, in a caressing motion.

Once petted, a baby seal is a difficult thing to get rid of. On all our other trips, we had been successful in eluding the infants. Today when we started for home the two petted seal babies followed. We went in and out of shallow passages thinking to lose them, only to discover a mile further that the two little seals were still following. We tied the boat, climbed out, and were on the path leading home.

"Look," said Lynn, "those god-damn seals are following. They're padding up the path behind us." We stopped. The two babies padded up to us and began to whine and mew.

"What'll we do?" I asked.

René patted a tiny head. "Let's take 'em home," he said. "Mamma will take care of 'em."

That's just what we did. Mamma didn't want the seals, but she fixed them some warm milk in the baby's unused bottle. We were amused to watch them suck the nipple.

"Now that they've eaten, you must put them overboard," she said.

We loaded the two babies into the wheelbarrow. Reaching a pool of deep water on the same side of the island as the seal rock, we carefully dropped the little puppylike creatures overboard. Then we ran. In a few hours they were crying around the back door.

Noel found the seals delightful company and played with them and petted them. From then on they were pests. Mamma called one Paddy, probably because he padded about with a lot of noise; the other, we named Flipper.

"You can't keep the god-damn pests around the lighthouse," said Papa. "I'll take them out to deep water and lose them."

Our tears were unheeded by both our parents.

"We just *can't* be bothered by seals around the house," argued Mamma. "Besides, they get pretty mean as they grow older. You're liable to be bitten."

Papa took the seals over by Sucia Island, about three miles away, and dropped them overboard.

One morning in the fall, when Mamma opened the back door, Flipper lay dead against the sill. There were no marks of violence on him. We couldn't guess what had happened.

Late that afternoon, Paddy returned. He was more of a pest than ever. The loss of his friend Flipper forced him to find companionship with us. He followed Mamma about the house, hanging onto her skirts and whining. He sounded just like a spoiled child. In vain, Mamma sent him away. She asked the owner of a fishing boat to take Paddy out into the strait and drop him overboard. Paddy returned that night. She sent him away again, on the *Elmo*. In a few days, he was back again.

As a last resort, Mamma induced the captain of the *Manzanita,* a government lighthouse tender that used to call occasionally in place of the *Heather,* to take the baby seal clear off to Astoria. Mamma hoped that Astoria, about two hundred and fifty miles, was too far away for Paddy to return. In about a month, we were awakened one morning by a sharp, staccato barking outside the window. Lynn went down to see what was causing the noise. It was . the astonishingly homing Paddy!

Mamma was exasperated. She said, "If you don't get rid of that seal, I'm going to have a nervous breakdown."

Papa didn't want Mamma to have a nervous breakdown. He needed her, he said, to write letters for him; to make up the little talks on character that he delivered to us; to scratch his back. Yes, Papa liked Mamma and needed her. So he took Paddy down to the water's edge. We heard a shot.

Paddy never bothered Mamma again. We were ordered to keep away from the seal rock. Mamma didn't want any more baby seals for pets.

The following November, on a beastly night, the wind howled like a wild thing. I got out of bed and fastened the storm blinds, closing the shutters tightly, hoping to shut out the noise.

Just before midnight, I heard the sound of running feet, and the squeak of an opening door. In a moment, Papa's voice boomed up the stairway. "Come on and help me—everybody!" he yelled.

I jumped out of bed and ran to the stairway. The boys were already sliding down the banister. I followed.

Mamma came down the stairs behind us. "What on earth—" she began.

"Birds," yelled Papa. "Millions of them—all over the tower!" He grabbed a lantern and lighted it. "Here, you kids run to the barn and get sacks—lots of them. Come to the fog signal." He was gone, followed by Mamma.

We hurried to the barn. Picking up all the sacks we could carry, we ran all the way to the fog signal.

"Gee," said René. "The light in the tower is out."

"Not all the way out," I said. "I can see a tiny bit of it."

"God-damn, shut up and run faster," said Lynn.

Upon opening the fog signal door, we gasped in surprise. Every where were little yellow canaries, hundreds and hundreds. They flew against the window panes, sat on the engine belt, the top of the windows. They swarmed all over the engines. The floor was covered with injured birds, flapping about miserably.

Mamma came down the tower steps. "Bring the sacks and follow," she said.

We climbed the stairs, carefully avoiding the canaries on the steps. The tower was a mess. The door was open; Papa was out on the balcony. Mamma took the sacks, motioning for us to follow. The entire tower was blanketed with canaries. Papa began to scrape them off into the sacks. The poor little things were too cold and weak to move.

"Blown off their course, and nearly frozen to death," said Papa. "Must have been blown all the way from California. Here, hold a sack." He scooped the yellow mass into the sacks as fast as he could work. "Now, take them to the barn and empty them out," he said.

Lynn and I each took one end of a sack. It wasn't very heavy. We carried it to the barn, and dumped the birds out. Closing the barn door, we returned for more. Several times we made the same trip, until the tower was freed of its "blanket".

"I hope no one on the mainland noticed my light was dark," worried Papa. "It was black for more than an hour. I'd hate to be reported." He was polishing the windows.

Inside the tower, Mamma was picking up the last of the birds. She helped Papa clean the feathers and dirt from the lens.

We waited in the fog signal until Papa and Mamma came down. We helped to gather all the birds we could catch, and carry them to the house.

"Put them in the woodshed," Papa ordered. There were still dozens and dozens of wounded birds in the fog signal.

It was morning before our work was done. We were too excited to sleep, so we dressed and went down to the barn to see how the canaries were.

The weather was still windy and freezing. Mamma didn't know what to do with the canaries. She fixed some boxes of chicken feed, put one in the barn and one in the woodshed. Then we filled pie tins with water, placing them where the birds could get them.

Papa and Al killed all the wounded canaries that were in the fog signal, and left the others alone.

"It's a mess, anyway," said Papa. "Better let them stay until the storm lets up."

Al prepared a feeding place for them on some newspapers.

For two days our strange guests rested on the island, waiting for a favorable wind. Finally, one calm morning they took off, flying toward the south.

Soon it was summer again, and with the coming of the salmon came Billy Coutts, just back from California. Billy always returned for the salmon fishing.

Curly was boisterous in his welcome, and so were we. Billy's coming always meant months of fun for the family.

There was a very fine resort hotel on Mayne Island, on the Canadian side of the channel. Once a month, the islanders were accustomed to gather in the hotel ballroom for an evening of dancing. Folks came from all the neighboring islands. Everyone brought food for the great midnight supper that followed the dance.

Our first introduction to the Mayne Island Ball was the occasion of the Queen's birthday, a holiday celebrated each year on May 24.

Billy Coutts invited Mamma, Papa, Al, Mary, Clara, Estelle, Lynn, René, and me to go to the dance with him.

"Is there room for so many on the *Sea Pigeon?*" asked Papa.

"Plenty of room for all," answered Billy. "I'll drop over to East Sound tonight and arrange with Mr. Stark to keep the lighthouse for that evening." Mr. Stark, a retired lighthouse keeper, often helped with the work when Papa was ill.

"Thank you," answered Papa. "We'll be ready at four o'clock Saturday afternoon."

All that week we hurried about, getting our best clothes ready for the ball. Mamma, Mary, Clara, and Estelle spent endless hours ironing starched ruffles of petticoats and other underthings, sewing on ribbons, frills, and beads.

Mamma and the big girls roasted several chickens, stuffed dozens of eggs, baked three lovely cakes and several recipes of cookies. They packed them all into baskets, to be carried to the dance.

On Saturday morning, Billy brought Mr. Stark, and Papa instructed him in the care of the station. At four o'clock we boarded the *Sea Pigeon* and sailed for Mayne Island.

It was a lovely trip. We sailed directly along the golden pathway made by the setting sun. As the evening shadows fell, everyone sang "Twilight Is Falling Over the Sea." There were other boats going our way; the voices of the passengers blended in the chorus of the song we were singing: "Far away, beyond the starlit skies..." When the song was ended, someone began "Santa Lucia." I shall always remember that night of splendor—the singing voices, the soft chugging of motors, the silvery swish of parting waters, and the purring whir of the night wind as we passed.

Upon arriving at the hotel, Papa carried the baskets of food to the kitchen. We were then escorted to our rooms to dress for the ball.

When we were assembled to go downstairs to the dance, I thought that we were a nice-looking family. I was especially thrilled when I looked at Mary. She was radiant. She wore a dress of white mull, with little bows of black velvet ribbon all over the full skirt. When Mary walked the dress swept out behind her, with a nice little swish caused by the taffeta ruffles on her petticoat. On the top of her hair, she had a bow of black watered taffeta ribbon, and another just like it at the back of her neck. The bows almost covered her blue-black hair. She used four yards of three-inch ribbon in each bow. Her feet were clad in black satin slippers with high heels. Oh, she was beautiful.

Clara and Estelle were pretty in their fluffy blue dresses, but Mamma was the prettiest of all. She wore a silvery blue gown that was embroidered with tiny pink and blue beads. Her hair was piled high on her head, the ends escaping in shoulder-length curls. Her fan was shell pink, with carved ivory handles.

"Mamma looks like a girl," I remarked.

"Mamma looks like a queen," answered Papa.

The ballroom was a large and beautiful room, high ceilinged and lighted with brilliant chandeliers. The musicians, four violinists and a pianist, were from Salt Springs. Their music was charming.

A large crowd was seated in the chairs that lined the walls of the ballroom.

"These people are your neighbors," Billy told us. "Some are country gentlemen, some remittance men (many of them titled), others farmers or laborers. They are all from the islands surrounding your Patos. There is one young man in particular whom I should like to present to Angie." He walked across the room, returning directly with a little boy about my own age.

"Angie, may I present Frankie?" Billy's eyes twinkled as he introduced us.

"How do you do?" I barely whispered.

"H'lo, Angie!" Frankie shouted back at me. From that moment we were friends.

There were several small girls and boys at the dance that night. My brothers and I had a good time with them. Papa had taught us to dance the Spanish waltz, the two-step, and the minuet. These we did creditably.

"You're a peachy dancer, Angie," whispered Frankie.

I danced with Papa, my brothers, Al, Billy, and Frankie. The orchestra played "Over the Waves," "Blue Danube," and "Minuet Don Juan." These were dreamy numbers; I was enchanted.

Once Mary waltzed by with a handsome young man.

"He's a young English nobleman. His name is Lord Maude," announced Billy, enviously eying Mary.

My heart pounded for Mary. She looked just like a radiant princess.

In between dances, we sat and fanned our faces. Everyone had fans, and as the men fanned their ladies there was presented a rich scene of ever moving color.

"Isn't the ball heavenly?" panted Estelle. "Billy is such a marvelous dancer."

"He has such charming ways," answered Clara. "Have you noticed how Mary rolls her eyes at him?"

"Yes," answered Estelle, "and Al doesn't look very happy about it."

I hadn't noticed Al, but now I watched. Estelle was right. He *didn't* look very happy.

My feet, encased in tight Mary Jane slippers, began to hurt. I sat down to rest. Frankie bowed before me. "May I have the pleasure?"

"Oh, you Canadian kids are too proper!" I scolded. "Don't you ever do nothin' but bow and dance and be polite? My feet hurt. I want to go out and walk on the beach."

"Let's," agreed Frankie.

Lynn and René had the same idea. We met outside the pavilion, and started off down the beach.

"Let's go wading," suggested Frankie.

We took off our shoes and stockings, and began to wade. After a few minutes of splashing about, the boys suggested taking our clothes off and riding the logs. Now, riding the logs was one of the greatest pleasures of my life. It was quite a trick to keep the logs from rolling over. We didn't mind a bit when we were rolled into the deep coolness of the water. So when the boys stripped, I stripped too. I hung my beautiful new dress on a stump, folded my underthings and laid them nearby. Soon we were all four paddling about on the logs in the moonlight.

"The music's stopped," announced René. "They'll be eating supper."

"We'd better get dressed," I said.

"What will you say to Mamma about your wet curls?" asked Lynn.

I couldn't think of a single thing to tell Mamma, and I began to wonder where my clothes were.

"I left them right here," I quavered. "Someone must've taken them."

"Frankie was up there while we were riding the logs," said Lynn. "Did you see anyone around, Frankie?"

"No, I didn't," said Frankie. "I didn't see anyone."

We searched and searched. I didn't have a thing to put on.

"What'll we do?" I asked. I was getting cold, and it was all I could do to keep from crying.

"I know," said Frankie, "we'll go in the back way.

There's a door leading to the dressing room. It's a secret door. Only I know about it."

We followed Frankie, my wet curls slapping me from behind with a clammy feeling.

"Now, when I push the door open," said Frankie, "you run like blazes, Angie. Run straight to the dressing room and no one will see you. No-o-o one at all." Laughing, Frankie pushed the door open and shoved me through.

I started to run, and then stopped dead. I had run directly into the center of the ballroom floor and everyone was staring at me! For one unbelieving instant I stood there, with one shoulder hunched up to my chin, wet curls dripping all about me. Then Mamma swooped down upon me and enveloped me in the folds of her best satin gown. She bore me away to the dressing room.

Mamma was mad. Her face was red as a beet. "What a horribly humiliating thing," she stormed. With her hand she blistered my bottom, right in front of the ladies who had trooped in to offer assistance.

Frankie's mother brought me a gown, and Mamma put me to bed. I wept and wept. I was almost sure that Frankie had taken my clothes and had planned the whole thing. What hurt most was the fact that no one remembered to bring me any supper at midnight.

All the way home, the next morning, there was gloom. Mamma

was mad at Papa for laughing about my strange escapade. Al was mad at Mary for flirting with Billy. Estelle was mad at everyone in general. She hadn't danced with Billy enough to suit her.

That evening, Papa called our regular Saturday evening conference. First they finished me off with a court martial. I was not to go to Mayne Island to the ball again all summer. I wanted to get even with someone, but I couldn't determine who.

Estelle took the floor next. "Mamma," she said, "Mary flirted terribly at the ball last night."

Mary sprang up. "Why—why—you—"

Al hastily rose and left the room. He was a West Pointer; his lady's honor was involved, and not wishing to defend her, he retreated.

Mary began to cry. "Oh, Mamma, I didn't. I didn't," she began.

Mamma stood up. "This is a question we will settle in private, Mary. Estelle, you will please keep your thoughts on the subject to yourself."

Then timid little Margaret raised her hand.

"Yes, Margaret," said Mamma.

"Mamma," she asked, "will you please put elastic in Thalia's panties so she can take care of herself at the toilet?" The request was granted, and Margaret was starry eyed. Thalia looked daggers at her.

Papa gave his customary little talk on character. "Tonight, we will dwell on *courage*," he announced. "'Sacrifice and courage go hand in hand,'" quoted Papa. "'We must face life with confidence. It will help us to endure whatever we have to go through—' blah, blah, blah, blah, blah," droned Papa's voice. I didn't care about courage. Courage indeed. It took all the courage I could muster to keep from crying right now. No more dances for a whole year. I'd like to get ahold of that Frankie!

After the meeting adjourned, I slipped out to the front porch and lay down under the parlor window. The window was open a bit, and I intended to hear what Mamma was going to say to Mary. They were talking now. Mamma's voice came clear and troubled.

"Mary, would you care to tell me what the trouble is?"

"Oh, Mamma, truly I didn't mean anything wrong," wept Mary. "The music was so romantic, and Billy dances so divinely and says the nicest things."

"Do you love Al?" asked Mamma.

"Oh—yes, I do," slowly answered Mary, "but I think he's more like a brother. It isn't that I don't love him, but he's so unattentive. He never brings me gifts any more, and sometimes I long for romance again—"

Mamma stopped her. "Mary, you are a very selfish woman. Al doesn't bring you gifts because he has to spend the money for other things that you demand. Didn't you just buy an expensive Victrola and a new rug? I'm ashamed of you, Mary. You want to eat your cake and have it, too. If you really love Al, you won't expect him to go on courting you. Love is a deeper thing than mere courtship. Courtship should end when marriage takes its place."

Mary interrupted. "I know, Mamma. Al loves me, and I think I love him, but it's different with Billy. My heart beats fast and little bells inside me begin to tinkle whenever I see him."

"Mary, promise me you'll be a good wife to Al. He's like a son to me, and good to you."

"Oh, I won't break my marriage vows," promised Mary, "even though it's like being married to my brother. If I could make him jealous, maybe—" Mamma cut her off.

"No, Mary, you are wrong. Jealousy leads only to heartache. You are treading on very dangerous ground. Let us end this talk with a prayer, and I want you to sleep over it tonight. Tomorrow you will see your error."

Mamma and Mary bowed their heads, and Mamma prayed.

"We thank Thee, Father, for the wisdom that is ever around us. Teach us to be humble, virtuous. And may our lives be purified by the richness of Thy understanding love. Through Jesus Christ, our Lord."

I didn't hear the rest, because Al had come quietly up the steps and grabbed me by the back of the neck. He jerked me off the porch.

"Eavesdropping is a detestable habit," he said.

Mary came running out and ran straight into Al's waiting arms.

The next morning, I just *happened* to be inside the boathouse when Al and Billy were talking by the landing. I couldn't *help* hearing what they were saying.

"You are a West Pointer, and I am a Navy officer," said Billy. "There is no field of honor on which this thing can be fought out. She is your wife. We both are bound to defend the honor of our lady. Tomorrow, I shall leave. You may keep the *Sea Pigeon* until she can be disposed of. You can pick her up in Bellingham after Thursday."

The two men shook hands. Billy stepped into his skiff, shoved off, and rowed out to the *Sea Pigeon*. In a few minutes, the launch putted out of the bay. Al still stood where Billy had left him. He watched the launch out of sight, then sank down on the rocks, buried his head in his arms, and sat very still.

Although this photograph of Active Cove on Patos Island was taken in the 1940s, it depicts a young girl approximately the same age Angie would have been when this tale was told. *Photo courtesy of Puget Sound Maritime Historical Society*

CHAPTER EIGHT

One morning Lynn picked up his rifle, calling, "Come on, I'm ready to go."

René and I joined him for our morning's excursion around the beaches. Curly tagged close to Lynn's heels. He had been taught to heel whenever anyone carried a gun.

We stopped by the smokehouse. René climbed up the ladder and brought down a smoked salmon; we liked to nibble as we walked. Reaching the Head-of-the-Bay, we stopped for a drink of water from the well in the garden.

"Fish sure makes me thirsty," said Lynn.

"Me, too," I gasped. "I could drink a barrel of water."

René was seated on a fallen tree. "Please bring me a drink!" he asked. I filled the dipper and carried it to him. "René gets tired," I said to Lynn, "awfully tired."

"Yes," he answered, letting Curly drink from the dipper.

"What would Mamma say if she knew that you let Curly do that?" I asked.

"Well, don't tell her just to find out," Lynn answered. We stopped again at the outside garden, and each of us picked a juicy head of cabbage.

"If we get thirsty from the salmon," Lynn said, "we can eat a mouthful of juicy cabbage."

We proceeded on our way, watching for the unusual on the shore. Somewhere Bully, the Holstein, was bellowing.

"Bull's loose; better keep close together," warned Lynn. His hand gripped the rifle. We weren't talking much now; the champing from three mouths crunching cabbage was all the noise we wanted. We had to listen for Bully.

As we neared the scrub oak, we were startled by a loud noise. We stood still and listened.

"Sounds like something splashing in the water," said Lynn. "Something big."

We quietly threaded our way through the scrub oak, taking pains to walk around a yellow jackets' nest. Lynn was the first to reach the opening in the brush, which afforded us a view of the harbor.

"God-damn!" he whispered. "Look!" We looked, our eyes wide with surprise. A seal was attacking a very large salmon.

Curly stalked up, tensely alert.

"Quiet, boy," commanded Lynn. Curly dropped to the ground and waited. He wouldn't make a move now until further command. We stood watching. The fight raged immediately inside the kelp bed.

Tossing the enormous salmon high into the air, the seal brought him down with a terrific spank. The water splashed high above the combatants. The salmon lashed back with his tail, striking the seal with resounding smacks, causing him to emit short grunts just like a pig.

It was a thrilling fight. The water all about them was covered with bloody foam.

"I hope the salmon wins," I said.

"I don't," answered René. "Seals have to have food to eat."

Lynn looked disgusted. "They don't have to kill off the salmon," he said. "They can eat bullheads, suckers, and seaweed." He raised his rifle. Curly stood up.

"I'm going to shoot that god-damn seal," Lynn said.

"No! No!" René protested. "Papa said not to shoot at seals—they're protected."

"Well, who's going to tattle to Papa?" asked Lynn, lowering his gun.

"I'm not," quavered René, "but Papa talked about obedience at last Saturday's conference."

"Oh, for hell sakes!" said Lynn. "Go on home and play with the little kids—you—you—*goody-goody!*"

He raised the rifle again. Curly watched. Just as Lynn pulled the trigger, the seal raised his body out of the water and tossed the great fish on high. Lynn's bullet struck the salmon. Both seal and salmon dropped out of sight.

"You hit the salmon," I shouted.

"I hit the seal!" screeched Lynn. "Lie down," he commanded Curly, whose whole body was quivering as he waited for the word "Fetch!"

Curly was disappointed. He was accustomed to fetch following the report of a gun. He lay down and whimpered softly.

"I'm going to tell Papa on you," I said. "You're not supposed to shoot seals *or* salmon, and you shot a salmon."

"I tell you I shot a seal!" shouted Lynn, "and if you want to be a tattletale, go on home—both of you go on home."

René and I ran down the bank and started up the trail toward home. Curly remained with Lynn. He was trained to follow the man with the gun.

We reached a point near the spring, and were entering a clearing, when all of a sudden we came face to face with Bully. We had forgotten all about him, and had been laughing and talking quite loud. We stopped dead in our tracks. Bully switched his tail, lowered his head, and rumbled. One foot began to paw the ground. I came to life.

"Come on, René," I said, tugging at René's cold hand. "Maybe we can reach the fence before he catches us!" We ran to the edge of the bank and quickly slid over, to land on a narrow path below. "Run fast," I said.

"I can't. I've got my pain again," wept René. His face was white and strained.

We both noticed that Bully had circled behind us and was picking his way down the rocks to our path. I tried to drag René. I couldn't lift him.

"Papa," I screamed. "Papa! Papa!"

Suddenly a rifle crack sounded and Bully roared and whirled. I looked up. There, above us, stood Lynn, his smoking gun in his hands. His shot had grazed Bully's nose.

"Get him, Curly!" he shouted to the eager dog. Curly hated Bully, and ran snarling after him. Bully charged up the bank, his hoofs pounding on the rocks as he pursued Lynn. Curly snapped at his heels, slowing him a little, allowing Lynn time to reach the brush and crawl through to the safety of the rocks below.

"I don't hurt now. I can walk," said René. We reached the fence and slid under, sitting down in the grass to wait for Lynn. He came picking his way along the slippery rocks. Once inside the fence, Lynn emitted a long-drawn-out whistle. "Can't let Curly get hooked," he said. The obedient dog returned in a few minutes. He was laughing. This was the first time he had been allowed to bite the bull.

"Lynn," said René, "we won't tell about the salmon."

"No," I added, "we'll tell Papa how you saved us." Lynn left his rifle on the ground to be picked up later. We crossed our arms and made a chair for René, and slowly carried him home.

Early in the spring, our great-grandparents, Grandpa and Grandma Lee, came to visit. Grandpa Lee was a close relative of Robert E. Lee, the Civil War hero, and looked exactly like him. He had white hair and blue eyes that looked out from under bushy brows. Grandpa Lee was very strict where children were concerned. He thought they should be seen and not heard. He was kind, though, and we liked him a lot.

Grandma Lee made us keep our hair combed and our faces washed.

"It isn't proper that a little girl should run about with boys," Grandma said. So she set about making a lady of me. She wanted me to learn to cook, sew, dust, and clean the lamp chimneys.

I hated housework in any form. I was an outdoor girl, and wanted nothing of the drudgery of the house.

Mamma and Papa took a little vacation while Grandma was there. They went to Seattle to a Shriners' convention.

Grandma was seventy-three years old, and had snow-white hair, which she piled high on her head in a mess that closely resembled a hen's nest. It was pretty hair; I wondered how it would look with a few eggs nesting in it.

In a day or so, Grandma had Margaret and me pretty well trained.

Grandma Lee taught me to help with the washing. She heated water in a wash boiler on the kitchen stove. Then she carried the hot water from the boiler, bucket by bucket, out to one of the tubs in the woodshed. This procedure was a long, drawn-out affair, requiring ten trips between kitchen and woodshed. (When Mamma did the washing, Papa and she carried the hot water out in one trip.) Grandma and I were home alone. The water was too heavy for her to carry, and I couldn't help much. Then Grandma carried cold water from the faucet outside on the tank house and put it into the second tub.

She got the washboard from its hook and, plopping a large bar of Mamma's yellow homemade soap in my hands, ordered me to begin. The water was too hot for my unaccustomed hands and the lye in the soap, coupled with the rubbing, soon had eaten the skin from large areas of both hands.

"Grandma," I wailed, "my hands are hurting."

"They'll be all right. Just a little skin rubbed off," she answered.

She took over the washing, ordering me to stay and watch. This I did for two solid hours while Grandma washed, rinsed, and "blued" the clothes.

"You may help me hang them out," she said.

My hands were very sore now, and seemed to be getting worse. The lye kept eating into my skin.

I began to hang up the smaller articles of the washing. I thought that I was doing a good job, when all of a sudden, Grandma screeched, "Fold those pants!"

Grandma had yelled "pants" right out loud. I was horrified. Mamma taught us to say "drawers" or "panties," and under no circumstances must we allude to these pieces of clothing in the presence of the boys. Grandma yelled the word so everyone could hear. Fortunately, the boys were away at the time.

The panties were of a peculiar type. They consisted of a narrow band on which were sewed two large cases like pillow slips, the bottoms of which had ruffles of homemade lace. Mamma always folded the cases together so they would resemble one pillow slip when hung to dry. She said that the boys must never know what they were.

This seemed silly to me because on the occasions when I had been swimming naked with the boys, I was sure that they had glimpsed my hidden panties hanging on a secluded bush. And I had heard the boys calling after the big girls in a teasing voice, "I see London, I see France, da—da—da—da—da—da—da—da." The girls always ran then, and squealed, and the boys laughed.

However, I folded them as Grandma ordered. After I had helped her carry the wash water out and poured it on the flower beds, Grandma told me I could go and play.

My hands were too stiff and sore for playing. They grew steadily worse. When I could no longer stand the pain, I ran to Mamma's forbidden medicine cabinet to find some salve to put on them. I grabbed a large jar of yellow salve and applied the stuff to my sore spots. After a few moments, I began to scream in earnest. The salve was a carbolic acid preparation that Mamma used for our wounds when we stepped on rusty nails. I ran screaming to Mary's house. She took one look, ran to the milk-house, brought back a large pan of thick cream, and plunged both my hands into it.

After a few weeks, my hands healed from the festered sores. Mamma said it was a wonder that they had been saved, and only because of Mary's quick action in treating them. No one said a word about the matter to poor Grandma Lee.

The wind was loud. It rattled the storm shutters all night. I hadn't been able to sleep. In the early dawn someone called my name. The room was dimly lit, in the gray morning, but I saw Lynn standing in the doorway.

"Come on," he whispered. "Be quiet, don't wake the others; we're going to watch the storm."

I quietly slipped out of bed, and in my nightgown followed him downstairs, mindful of the step that creaked (although the storm was so loud that I didn't think Mamma would hear wild horses on the stairs).

At the front door, we were joined by René. We stepped out into the gray storm. Unmindful that we were clad only in our night-clothes, we joined hands and ran to the bank overlooking the tossing sea. The waves were dashing high, sending white spray over every-thing. We hung closely together in the gale, for fear of being washed overboard. Reaching our favorite pine tree, which was gnarled from many such storms, and whose roots were so deeply embedded in the rocks that no storm could tear it loose, we sat down to watch the fury of the wind and waves.

It was a fearful sight. Huge waves dashed far up on the rocks, leaving a wake of silvery white foam as they receded. The wind screamed furiously and whistled, pushing the sea into new fury. The angry sea slapped back at the wind, fiercely trying to catch it (as if it ever could).

In a cove, a short distance away, we could see large white beach logs being tossed high into the air—to go crashing, end over end, back into the sea.

The kelp beds were ravaged. Giant kelp heads standing on their tails were dancing back and forth together, like weird creatures out of witch tales. Their long ribbons, streaming far out behind them in the wind, resembled ghost robes. It was an eerie sight.

Farther out from shore where the large swells rose and fell rhyth-mically, huge snowy sea gulls rode the crests of the waves. It looked like fun. I wished I could be out there with them.

As morning broke, the storm grew a little less violent, so we left our pine tree to go exploring the rocky shoreline, anxious to see what the ebbing tide had washed up in its fury. In a small pool of water we found dozens of tiny, spotted fish swimming. They were imprisoned until the change of tide should liberate them. Today, we were too excited to pay much attention to the little fish. We were looking for larger, much more exciting victims of the storm.

We rounded a point of land and began to explore a lagoon that had always afforded us a great deal of pleasure. Today we were gratified. Here, in shallow water, lay a large octopus.

Screaming with delight, we scrambled back to the beach to hunt for sharp poles with which to torment him. This was great sport to our wild, cruel young natures. We found suitable poles, and returned to the lagoon. We lunged at the huge creature, sticking our sharp poles into his body. The eight long arms tossed and curved in a most frightful manner. We laughed in fiendish glee. We failed to notice that at each thrust of our poles the octopus had moved a little nearer to where we stood in the water.

Our danger dawned upon us suddenly when the octopus, with a slow, snakelight twist, wrapped one long, sucking tentacle around my leg! I pulled, and thrust my pole into his beaklike face, but I couldn't get away. The horrible, sticky, squeezing arm sucked tight to my leg, and then two, and three more tentacles encircled me, up under my nightgown and around my body. I thought my skin was being torn away and surely I should be squeezed to death.

"Oh-o-o-o-h!" I screamed in terror.

Lynn still fought the octopus. I turned to see why René wasn't helping. He was gone. I began to sob, "Oh, God, God, help me!" I noticed that the octopus was retreating toward deeper waters, pulling me with him.

Lynn fought valiantly. "Don't let him drag you down!" he shouted. "Keep from falling!"

When the water was up past my waist, Lynn began to scream with me. The octopus just about had me submerged when I heard a shout and Papa, followed by René, appeared around the point. Papa hastily hacked at the tentacles with a long dagger, freeing me. What remained of the octopus slid into the deep water and dropped from sight.

Papa carried me home. He didn't speak a word all the way. Once inside the house, he removed my wet gown and, placing me in a convenient position, gave me a spanking that has never been erased from my memory. He then did the same for Lynn. We were glad that René was spared any punishment.

When Mamma had given me some bitter medicine and had me in a warm bed, she sat down beside me. "Now, I suppose you know that you were nearly drowned today," she said, "and I hope you realize that I am not the least sympathetic with you."

"Why, Mamma," I said, "don't you love me at all?"

"That is not the issue. You were torturing a poor creature," she said, "and you got just what you deserved."

I knew Mamma was right. I hated the octopus, but I had provoked the attack.

As soon as I had recovered sufficiently to be up and around I sought out God. "Why didn't you help me when the octopus had me?" I asked.

"I didn't know that an octopus would attack a child," countered God. "Just what happened?"

"You know what happened," I said. "You know everything. You saw me poking him with a stick."

"There's the answer to your question," said God. "You were tormenting one of my creatures. You deserved what you got."

I pulled up my dress and showed God the scars where the skin had become festered.

"Just look," I said. "Don't you feel sorry at all?"

"Yes, I do," sighed God. "I'm always sorry when sinners hurt themselves by their own folly."

I covered up my wounds and slowly walked away from God. I was thoroughly ashamed. I have never forgotten the lesson. From that day on, I have had a deep compassion for all creatures.

Colonel Theodore "Teddy" Roosevelt, 26th President of the United States (1901–1909) and visitor to Patos Island. *Photo by Underwood & Underwood*

CHAPTER NINE

One warm day when I was sleeping in the hayloft, I was awakened by the sound of Papa's loud voice coming from the stall beneath me. He was talking to Al, who was milking a cow in the next stall.

"How are you and Mary making out?" asked Papa.

"In what way?" asked Al.

"The way of the heart," answered Papa. "I just wondered if she was treating you the way a good wife should treat her husband."

Al didn't answer at once. I peeked through a crack in the floor. His head was pressed tight against the cow's belly. He was stripping the udders slowly and thoughtfully. Finally he said, "If you don't mind, Dad, what goes on between my wife and me is strictly my own business."

"I didn't mean to pry," said Papa, "but it seems to me there should be some grandchildren coming along. Let's see—you've been married about four years—"

"Grandchildren!" exclaimed Al. "It seems to me that there are enough children around here as it is. You've seen to that. Besides, I have all I can do to help care for *your* brood. Don't talk to me about grandchildren."

"It isn't the same," said Papa. "You should have a few of your own to carry on your name. Now, if you want me to talk to Mary—I might warm her up a—"

"That's enough!" said Al. He stood up and turned toward Papa.

"Keep your thoughts to yourself. I refuse to discuss my wife with anyone."

"Hell," said Papa, "I just want to help you. I had the same trouble. You have to know how to handle a cold wife. Now the French—"

"Shut up!" shouted Al. "I'll not listen to a word against Mother. Cold? With thirteen kids? Why, you old stud horse!" He picked up his pail of milk and dumped it on Papa's head.

"Damn-it-to-hell," shouted Papa, "what did you do that for? You god-damn fool."

Al was almost out of the barn door. He turned. "And that's another thing—that swearing. You do it in front of the ladies and children. I'm getting sick of it. It shows a lack of vocabulary. Why don't you get next to yourself?"

Papa was just standing there, completely dumfounded. I felt sorry for him. I didn't think he looked a bit like a horse. Especially like Bill, our plow horse, who the boys said was a stud.

After dinner Papa and Al were down by the fog signal. I wanted to hear what they were saying, so I crept around behind the oil house.

"It's all right," said Papa. "I had it coming."

"I'm sorry," said Al. "I just can't stand vulgarity. I know that you are a good man, Dad. You just haven't had the breaks. No one took the trouble to teach you chivalry."

"Chivalry, hell!" said Papa. "I'm noted for my chivalry. What the hell you talking about?"

Al threw his hands over his head.

"Good night, Dad," he said.

In June, Papa received a letter from Colonel Roosevelt. He had recently returned from a hunting trip in Africa, and was intending to make a speaking tour in the West. Later in the summer, he would pay us a visit.

The news threw the family into a state of joyful anticipation. We were all fond of the Colonel, although we children had never met him.

CHAPTER NINE ∾

"We'll paint the whole place," said Papa, "and whitewash the barn and sheds." He immediately began to carry out his plans.

For the next three weeks, the household was in a state of frenzied confusion. The guest room was scrubbed until it shone like a mirror; the floor was freshly painted, and the rug cleaned. Mamma took down the butterfly chamber that had belonged to Grandpa Lee and polished it brightly, as she did the water pitcher and bowl. Our second-best lamp was polished, and Papa brought from the fog signal a new wick and chimney.

A week before the scheduled visit, Papa, Al, and Roy had finished painting the fog signal, tower, and house. During the painting of the tower, Roy had crushed his lame knee between a scaffolding and the building. He limped so badly that Papa excused him from further work. So Roy helped about the house. He polished the silver and wrapped it in flannel. The barn and chicken house gleamed in their new coats of whitewash. Two days before the Colonel arrived, Mamma and Mary baked dozens of cookies to fill the stone crocks in the pantry. Papa killed a goose, and we children prepared it for roasting.

We were all dressed in our finest clothes, and gathered at the boathouse when the white yacht *Dawn* came dancing into the bay. Her davits were swung out, and the small boat was lowered.

"There he is!" Papa cried, as the Colonel seated himself in the boat. Papa and Mamma walked to the water's edge.

When the small boat touched shore, the Colonel quickly stepped out and, in a moment, the great man and Papa were hugging each other and uttering sounds suspiciously like those uttered by bears.

"Awa-a-rr-r," groaned Papa in ecstasy.

"Wa-aa-ar-r," roared the Colonel. He unwound himself and shook hands with Mamma.

The greetings over, Papa brought the Colonel to the top of the steps and introduced him to his long line of children.

"This is Roy, Mary, Al, Clara, Estelle, Lynn, René, Angie, Margaret, Thalia, and Noel," said Papa.

"Whew," whistled the Colonel, looking around to see if there were any more. Curly edged up; the great man's hand slid over the dog's ears. "Nice work, Cap'n," he said. "Large families are a blessing to our country."

The procession moved along the boardwalk in the direction of the house.

"You really have a little paradise here, Cap'n; a good place to hide out for a much-needed rest."

Mamma showed the Colonel to his room. "My, my!" exclaimed the Colonel. "Who is the naturalist?"

Mamma looked into the bedroom and gasped. Across and all around the walls and ceiling were strung *all* of my strings of sea pigeons' eggs. On the washstand and bureau lay my collection of starfish, sea urchins, and the back of a highly shellacked king crab. On the bed, elegant in a red ribbon necktie, sat my precious teddy bear; on the wall, over the head of the bed, hung a beautiful stuffed owl—Nothing was too good for the Colonel.

As I hastily slid down the banister, I heard Mamma wail, "Oh, that Angie; she'll be the death of me yet!"

This remark was followed by a roaring laugh from the Colonel.

For two days, the Colonel visited with Papa. He inspected the fog signal, walked around the beaches, and played with the children. He fished for, and caught, a ninety-pound *tyee* salmon. But most of the time, he and Papa talked politics. Papa always roared and hit the table with his fist when he talked politics. It always frightened me, and I wished they didn't have to have politics.

Mamma forever took advantage of any opportunity to show off Estelle's elocutionary accomplishments. She did so at this time. At dinner, she brought up the subject of her dramatic ability and, as the conversation progressed, acquainted the Colonel with the fact that Estelle could recite very nicely. The Colonel expressed a desire to hear Estelle during the evening. When the dishes were washed and carefully stacked away in the pantry, we gathered in the parlor. Papa and the Colonel sat side by side—the distinguished man and the lowly lighthouse keeper—their mustaches crooked in the same odd manner.

The Colonel asked Thalia to sit on his knee.

"No," said the bashful child.

"Why not?" asked the Colonel.

"I'm afwaid," answered Thalia. "Papa and you look just like a walwus!"

After the Colonel had told us stories of his recent hunting trip in Africa, he asked Estelle to recite for him. Estelle proudly walked to the center of the room, firmly braced her feet, and stood very straight. In an unnatural pose she began, in a singsong voice, "I will recite 'Bingen on the Rhine.'"

"A *soldier* of the *legion*, lay *dying* in Al*giers,*" Estelle recited. She bent on one knee, timing her action to the rhythm, and tapped the air with one fist, in very dramatic style. When she reached the part where:

> A comrade stood beside him
> As his life blood ebbed away;
> And knelt, in pitying silence
> To hear what he did say—

we younger children burst into tears and were asked to leave the room, to return when the selection was ended.

After Estelle finished her sad recital, the Colonel asked her to do another.

Estelle beamed, "I will recite 'Curfew Shall Not Ring Tonight.'"

We listened without tears this time, as Estelle dipped, whirled, bucked, and waved her arms through the morbid tale about the harshness of Cromwell, and the curfew that must not ring. We listened, breathless, while Estelle alternately became Bessie, the pleading sweetheart of the boy condemned to die at the ringing of the curfew, and the stern Cromwell. We followed Estelle up the steep tower steps, as she depicted Bessie. With Bessie, we swung back and forth, clinging to the clapper of the curfew bell.

When she neared the end of her selection, Estelle stood in her best military portrayal of Cromwell, as she pointed her finger at the trembling Bessie and tensely and loudly emoted:

> "Go, your liver loves!" said Cromwell,
> "Curfew shall not ring tonight!"

Everyone began to laugh uproariously. Poor Estelle stood, unbelieving and shocked, in the middle of the room. Then, as the assembly roared anew, she rushed from the room in tears. The Colonel went after her, and soon had her laughing with the others.

Before the evening was over, everyone had an opportunity to "show off" to the Colonel. Papa loved to sing old songs, and tonight, for memory's sake, he suggested singing, "Remember the Maine."

"I'll sing with you," volunteered the Colonel. Papa and the Colonel sang:

> "When the vengeance wakes,
> and the battle breaks,
> "And the ships float out to sea,
> "When it's deck to deck ...
> "Remember the Maine."

Papa sang the tune and the Colonel sang the words.

"The Colonel needs a basket to carry his tune in," said Lynn.

"But he sings nice and loud," I answered.

It was a sad melody, and there were tears in the Colonel's eyes when the song was finished.

The Colonel was a wonderful man. He gave a little talk to the boys about democracy. He ended with: "The principle of democracy is virtue." He talked to the boys about good sportsmanship, and the value of accomplishing a good day's work.

"You must play the game earnestly," he said. "Play according to the rules, whether winning or losing—and play till the game is ended." He called their attention to the poem by Carlyle:

So here hath been dawning
Another blue day:
Think, wilt thou let it
Slip, useless, away?

"Never be ashamed of any honest work," he said. "Work is the most valued thing in a man's life."

We all wept when the Colonel left the island. Papa had many distinguished visitors, but never one to equal the Colonel.

Angie's home, the keeper's residence, on Patos Island circa 1910. Her father is on the right side of the porch. *Photo courtesy of Coast Guard Museum Northwest*

CHAPTER TEN

I n September Mamma sent the boys to school in Bellingham. "Young people should be with other young people," she said. Life on the island was very lonesome for me after they had gone. I hardly knew what to do with myself. Margaret didn't care for the wild sort of things that interested me; she preferred more ladylike pastimes, such as playing with dolls and reading books. Thalia was six, too young to play with me, as also was baby Noel. I was entirely alone.

Attempting to adjust myself to my solitary life, I began to walk about the beaches with Curly, seeking some sort of amusement.

One morning, I found a dead sea gull lying in the surf at the water's edge. It was a beautiful bird, large and snowy white, with faintly blue wings. Carrying the sea gull to a spot far from the water, I laid it on the grass.

"Why did you die?" I asked the dead gull. Then, remembering the stories about the healing powers of faith depicted in the Bible, I said, "I'll bring you back to life!"

I carried the dead bird to my prayer tree where for several hours I sat and prayed over him, using all the Bible phrases I could remember. Finally, feeling that I had prayed sufficiently, I began to enjoin the gull:

"Arise, take up thy bed and walk!" Still no move on the part of the gull. Again I prayed, "Oh, God, please make this perfectly good sea gull alive again. Amen."

Still getting no results, I repeated some more Bible words. "Weep not, she is not dead, but sleepeth," then, "Maid, arise!" The sea gull didn't move.

"Maybe it's a boy gull," I said aloud.

After a few moments, I put both hands on the sea gull. "Arise! Thy faith has made thee whole." Still the bird lay in quiet death.

"Oh, I guess he hasn't any faith," I said. "I'll give him a little boost." I went out of the prayer tree and tossed the sea gull high into the air.

"Fly, thou perfect image and likeness of a living gull." The gull fell to earth with a sickening thud.

"Oh, God!" I wailed. "You helped the fallen sparrows; why don't you help this beautiful sea gull? He's prettier than a sparrow."

I sat for a moment and pondered over my inability to raise the gull from death.

"Maybe God's mad at sea gulls because they scream so loud when we're having Sunday school. I'll bury him, and let God pull him out on Judgment Day. I'll go and get a shovel."

When I returned with the shovel, God was standing near my prayer tree. He was looking down at the dead sea gull. His eyes looked sad.

"Why didn't you revive him?" I asked.

"You should never pray to God the way you did, Angel," he answered. "God has reasons for everything He does. Perhaps this gull should die for a while."

"You're God—you could save him. Why don't you make him alive right now? I believe in you. You said in the Bible that if we believe enough, dead things will live again."

"Perhaps I will make him alive, but in my own way.

What are you doing with the shovel?"

"I was going to bury him."

"Don't bury him," God said. "He wouldn't want to be confined in a dark underground grave; a sea gull would want to fly free."

"How can he fly free, when he's dead?"

"I'll revive him, but first you have to cremate him. Then, when the ashes are cold, toss them out over the water, when the wind is blowing."

"What's cremate?" I asked.

"Ask Al," answered God. "Al will help you cremate him. Then when you toss the ashes on the tide, your sea gull will lift himself from death and go soaring away.

"Thank you, God," I cried as I picked up the dead gull and went in search of Al.

Al was down on the rocks behind the fog signal He was gazing dreamily out over the sound. I interrupted his daydream.

"Al, what's cremate?"

"It means to burn," answered Al. "Why do you ask?" I put the dead gull down beside him. "God told me to cremate this gull so he could go sailing away on the tide, and be free," I answered.

"I'd give anything to know where you get all your weird ideas, Angel; but if you think this gull would be happier cremated, why, we'll cremate him—at least it's a sanitary way of getting rid of him."

I followed him to the fog signal where he got an empty oil can; then to the oil house where he picked up a can of kerosene and some oily engine wipers. We walked back to the beach where the sea gull lay.

"We have to put him in the can, and cover it tightly. Then we'll build a fire in a hole in the rocks, and put the can over the fire. You go and gather some dry driftwood, while I soak these rags with the oil."

"Burn him?" I yelled. "No, don't burn himl"

"That's the way to cremate, Angel. Then he'll be silver ashes and you can throw them out over the tide rips and he can go wherever he wants to."

It all sounded so nice when Al explained it that I wiped my eyes and ran off to find dry pieces of driftwood for the fire.

"Now the fire's good and hot; we'll place the can in it." Al talked as he heaped the hot coals around the sides of the oil can.

"After the fire dies down, and the can cools off, you can scoop out the ashes."

I watched until the oil can was red hot; then I began to cry.

"This is no occasion for tears, but rejoicing," said Al. "Your gull will be free of his dead body. We'll go away, and come back in a few hours."

"Poor gull!" I sobbed. I took Al's hand and we walked up the little path that led through the wild roses to the group of shade trees in the orchard. Here we joined the rest of the family, and I became so engrossed in playing games that I forgot the cremation for a while.

It was several hours before I returned to the beach. I found the can—all whitened by the heat of the fire. When I opened it I saw only a fine white powdery substance. "Poor little gull!" I whispered. I scooped up the ashes in my hands, and running to the water's edge I tossed them out on the ripples.

"White wings spread out over the sea; fly little sea gull, forever floating free!" I chanted.

A whispering breeze caught the ashes, and dusted them over the dancing ripples just as a stray sunbeam flashed a bright smile on the water. From somewhere far out I heard a sea gull's joyous call, and as I watched the ashes go dancing out into the tide I whispered, "Forever—floating—free."

That night I heard Papa, Mamma, and Al talking about me.

"Let her alone, with her visions and voices," Al was saying. "She'll come out of it as she grows older. As I see it, she is so sold on the whole idea of religion that she conjures up a personal God to her own liking. Her belief is so great that she thinks she actually sees this mind image.

"I'd advise the family to ignore the whole business. Stop ridiculing and chiding her. It wouldn't hurt the rest of us to practice a little Christianity. Who knows: If we *all believe* a little more faithfully, perhaps we can all actually 'see' Angel's God."

"Well spoken!" roared Papa. "I always said that only those who honestly believe in God will ever see Him. I'll make the other children quit pestering Angel, and keep away from her prayer tree. All of them. If I ever hear of them going up there I'll skin them alive!"

The boys were home for Thanksgiving holidays. Together, we were patrolling the beaches.

"There were four sections yesterday," said Lynn. "I'm sure of it." We were standing on the bank, overlooking the log boom.

"Yes," I admitted, "I didn't see anything wrong with the raft yesterday."

"Let's go down," said René. "Maybe it just *looks* like there's only three sections."

We slid down the bank and walked to the boom. Climbing on the logs, we walked over the entire raft. There were only three sections, where there should have been four.

"Maybe the log patrol came last night and towed them away," suggested René. We hadn't heard Papa refer to this fact, but he could have forgotten to mention it.

We played a while on the logs, running back and forth over them quickly, taking care to keep the logs from rolling. This was accomplished by stepping on the top of each log as we passed. One day Lynn missed, and fell overboard, striking his head on a log as he went. When he came up, René grabbed him, but before we could haul him out, he had almost drowned.

We tired of "running the boom," as we called it, and started on our way home. We wanted to report the missing section to Papa.

"No," said Papa, "the patrol hasn't been down here. Someone must be stealing the logs." He talked it over with Al, and they planned to go down after dark to watch the raft.

"Let us go, too," we urged.

"All right, but you'll be up pretty late," said Papa.

Night came. Papa left Mamma in charge of the lighthouse. Carrying a lantern and some blankets, we three and Curly, with Papa, who carried his megaphone, and Al, who carried a gun, walked quietly down the path to the little harbor where the raft was anchored.

We sat in the stillness of the night for several hours, whispering and watching the night hawks. A loon cried, off somewhere in the distance. It was a cry that always made the back of my head cold. I shivered.

"Sh-h-h," whispered Papa. "I hear the pounding of a motor." We listened.

"Yes, I can hear it, too," whispered Lynn. Then we all heard the soft chug-chug of an engine. We waited in silence.

It was about midnight when Lynn nudged me awake. "Here they come," he whispered. Papa and Al were already standing behind trees at the edge of the bank.

"You kids get behind that stump," warned Papa in a whisper, "and stay there. Voices carry so at night."

We crawled behind the stump and peeked around the side. The large launch was drifting in, her motor silenced. She came right up to the raft.

Papa lifted his megaphone to his mouth. "Ahoy," he shouted, "the black launch! What is your business?"

There was no answer.

Again Papa shouted. "Ship ahoy! The black launch. This is government property. I'll give you one minute to get off!"

There was no movement on the launch.

"Fire on them," Papa commanded. Al raised the rifle and fired over the launch. Instantly there was a roar, as the engine started. The boat backed out, and in a minute had disappeared around the point.

"Log pirates. Let's go around to see if they pull in somewhere," said Papa. The men walked around the point. In a short while they returned.

"Come on," said Papa. "They're going like hell. I guess we scared the stuffing out of them."

All the way home, I shivered. That was the last time we ever lost any logs.

With December came the holiday season, bringing its noisy preparations for Christmas. The young people returned from school.

CHAPTER TEN ‿

It was after the Christmas festivities when Mamma noticed that René wasn't well. He sat, huddled up in the Morris chair, not caring for his Christmas books and games.

"Are you ill?" Mamma asked him.

"I have a terrible stomach ache, Mamma," he answered.

"Perhaps you've eaten too much," Mamma suggested. "The stomach ache will be better soon."

But René's stomach ache didn't get better that day, and during the night he began to scream from the acute pain he was suffering. Mamma hastened to his bedside.

She noticed the drawn-up knees and contorted face. "Appendicitis," she said.

We summoned Papa. He and Mamma determined what must be done. Papa took the ax and chopped some ice from the frozen-rain-water barrel that stood outside at the corner of the house. Mamma wrapped the ice in a towel and applied it to René's abdomen. Poor René cried out in agony.

"It's three days before the *Elmo* arrives," said Papa, "and the launch can't go out in this storm."

"Whatever shall we do?" asked Mamma.

"I can try a distress signal," Papa replied.

For three anxious days Papa watched for a ship to pass. It was blustery weather, and no ship appeared.

The storm still raged on Monday, preventing the *Elmo* from reaching the island. Mamma and Mary were sick with fear for René. They worked over him incessantly to make him as comfortable as possible.

René just lay and moaned. He didn't want any of us children to come near him.

"Mamma," he asked, "please read to me about Jesus."

Mamma read from *A Child's Life of Christ*. When she had finished, René spoke.

"I wish Jesus would take me away with Him. I'm so tired of this pain, Mamma—I've had it for so many years."

Mamma wept. "I didn't realize it was so bad, dear. I thought it was just a pain caused by running too fast."

"Mamma," I said, "René's pain didn't ever go away when he spit under a rock. Lynn's and mine did, but René's never did."

"I didn't know," sobbed Mamma. "I didn't know!" On the fifth day of René's illness, the storm let up, and the *Elmo* steamed into the bay. Papa carried René, wrapped in a blanket, to the ship. Mamma followed, and the three departed for Bellingham and the doctor.

We were a sorrowful group of children who waited that whole week for word of René's condition. Mary and the other big children tried to comfort us, but there was nothing that could console us. Lynn and I needed René. He was our confidant.

On Monday, we were waiting at the boathouse when the *Elmo* rushed into the bay. When Al rowed the boat out to receive the mail sack, we saw Papa and Mamma climb into it.

"Where's René?" we all wondered together.

When the boat touched shore, Mamma hastily climbed out. Putting her handkerchief over her face, she mumbled, "You tell them, Ed," and dashed past us up the steps to the walk.

Papa didn't soften the blow—he bluntly said, "René won't be back; he's dead."

For a moment, I stood like one turned to stone. Then, as the import of Papa's words penetrated my consciousness, I cried out, "No—no. It can't be true. Not René—not *dead!*" I began to run. Over the icy ground I ran until I fell exhausted under the leafless branches of Big Mad, the old madroña. Here I sobbed until I could sob no more.

"Oh, God, why did you do it? Why did you take him?" I asked.

I didn't feel that God was listening, so I got up and walked down the path to my prie-dieu. Falling to my knees on my prayer bench, I prayed, "Please, God, be kind to René in heaven."

And soft and low, God answered, "René is with Jesus. He is very happy."

During my walk home, I remembered René's words when he lay so ill. "I wish Jesus would take me."

At home, there prevailed a quiet gloom. Not seeing Lynn about, I went in search of him. After a while, I found him lying in the hay in the barn loft.

"Lynn," I began, "René wanted to go to Jesus—remember—"

"Get out of here," wailed Lynn. "Go away, Angie. Go away!"

I walked slowly home.

After several days had gone by, and René's belongings had all been put away, Papa told us what had happened at the hospital.

"We took him in," began Papa, "but we were too late. His appendix had ruptured; gangrene had set in. He died on the operating table."

"He lies in the cemetery at Bellingham," said Mamma. "He is safe in the arms of Jesus."

"Jesus!" I screamed. "I don't believe in Jesus—I hate Him!" Running out, I went to the old, gnarled tree in the scrub oak at Frustration's Rendezvous and cried.

"All you poor dead Chinese boys—just like my René." I wept until I was exhausted.

Then I heard someone say, "Don't cry, Angel. Everything's—all—right."

I looked around. There was no one in sight.

"I surely heard someone speak. God sure does get around without anyone seeing him," I thought.

Patos Island Lighthouse and keeper's residence circa 1920. *Photo courtesy of Puget Sound Maritime Historical Society*

CHAPTER ELEVEN

I awakened with a start. Someone had spoken to me.
"Oh, no!" I cried. "Not Florabelle." I hastily dressed and ran downstairs.

Mamma was frying the bacon for breakfast. She looked up as I rushed into the kitchen.

"Has Papa gone after her?" I tearfully asked. Mamma looked surprised.

"Gone after whom?" Mamma acted as if she didn't know what I was talking about.

"Why, Mamma," I said, "you just came to my room and said, 'Angie, Florabelle is overboard at the outside garden.'"

"I said no such thing, Angie. I haven't been out of this kitchen for an hour. You must have been dreaming."

"But, Mamma, I heard you. I—" I turned and ran, grabbing my jacket from its hook in the woodshed on passing through.

"Florabelle is overboard. Florabelle is overboard!"

The ugly words repeated themselves over and over in my mind.

"Someone spoke them," I said aloud, speeding down the path. Passing the barnyard, I noticed that neither Florabelle nor Charm was with the herd. Al was pouring water into the trough in the goose pen.

"Where to, so early?" he asked.

Not knowing why, I answered, "Florabelle's overboard." I ran on.

Before reaching the outside garden, I heard a cow bawling. It was urgent, high, and plaintive. I quickened my speed. I passed the garden and walked on around the point. There, on a sloping meadow, stood Charm. Her feet were braced far apart, and from time to time she glanced toward the sea and mooed.

The small streams of water that normally flowed from the hillside back of the slope had frozen over, making an almost solid sheet of ice over the entire meadow. Charm was standing in the ice, not daring to move lest she slide overboard.

Walking closer, I said, "Charm."

She moved her eyes in my direction, then cast them over the sea again. Florabelle was nowhere in sight. This was an unusual situation, as Florabelle and Charm were inseparable chums. Again the words ran through my mind, "Florabelle's overboard." Crawling on my hands and knees, I crept to the edge of the bluff. There, thirty feet below on a large flat rock in the water, lay Florabelle.

"Florabelle," I called.

She looked up, then lowered her head again as if looking up had caused her great pain.

Crawling back to safety, I took to the path and started for help. A short way down the trail, I met Al. "Did you find her?" he asked.

"Yes, she's overboard, and Charm is stuck in the ice. If she moves, she'll go overboard too."

Al turned back with me. "We'll have to get help," he said.

I went for Papa and some ropes, while Al launched the motorboat.

"Papa," I cried, "Florabelle's overboard, and Charm is stranded in the ice. Al's taking the launch around; he wants you to bring some rope and walk around to the bluff."

Papa ran to the house. I saw him come out the door a few minutes later. He was sticking something into his pocket. It looked suspiciously like a revolver. I shuddered. Together we quickly made the trip back to the bluff.

Papa made a lariat. "We'll try to pull Charm out," he said.

He threw the lariat, hoping to lasso Charm. The rope fell short, frightening her. She tried to scramble up the hillside, her hoofs ringing on the ice. It was only a moment, but to me it seemed like an eternity that Charm's hoofs dug at the icy sheet. Then she slid, clambering and sprawling, over the bluff.

The motorboat was approaching the rock where the two heifers lay. Papa and I picked our way down the treacherous cliff. Al reached the heifers, climbed out of the boat, and examined them.

Papa reached the rock and stooped over Charm. "She's hurt pretty bad," he said.

"This one, too," said Al.

Papa turned. "Angie, you'd better go home," he said.

I didn't want to leave. I wanted to pet Florabelle—to comfort her. I turned my back and began to climb up the rocks.

"Bang," and then—"Bang!" I whirled around. Both heifers lay stretched out on the rock.

"Papa," I shrieked, "you shot Florabelle and Charm! Oh, Papa! Papa!" I broke out in wild sobbing as I ran to the rock.

"Angie," said Al, "all four of Florabelle's legs are broken. We had to put her out of her misery."

"Now, run on home, Angel," commanded Papa. "We have to skin the calves."

I turned, and somehow in spite of blinding tears climbed up the rocks. At the top, I turned and looked back. They were skinning my pet, my darling Florabelle!

I didn't remember how I got home. I went straight to bed, numb with grief. "Oh, if only I'd die," I moaned.

Someone spoke, softly. "It's all right, Angel. It's all right."

"No, Mamma," I sobbed, "it's awful."

I turned to tell Mamma the horrible details. There was no one in the room!

Later I talked to God about Florabelle and Charm.

"I heard a voice," I said. "It told me that Florabelle was overboard. Mamma said it was intuition."

"Or perhaps mental telepathy," said God.

A few days later, I happened to go to the boathouse for my toy boats. There, rolled up and lying on the deck of the launch, were the skins of the two heifers. I fled in terror. Never before had the sight of a cow's hide bothered me, but from that day on, I could never bear to look upon the hide of any animal and for many years I was haunted by that small bundle of brown and white that I had seen that day in the boathouse.

In the early spring Mamma and Papa quarreled, and Mamma left home. No one knew exactly why Mamma was mad at Papa, but it had something to do with a recent trip to Florida with Colonel Roosevelt, and a perfumed handkerchief which Mamma had found in his coat pocket when he returned home. Anyway, she was mad, and she packed up her things and went to Seattle.

Papa felt terrible about the whole affair. "Now, why did she have to do a thing like that?" he asked. "I didn't do a thing, and she runs off and leaves me here with all you youngsters."

I felt sorry for Papa. He really needed Mamma. He went about in a melancholy mood, not wishing to talk. Margaret and I kept house as well as we could.

When Mamma had been gone for a week, and hadn't returned on the *Elmo's* last trip, Papa asked me to write a letter to her for him. This is what he wrote:

Dear Angel,

If you will come home, I will tell you the truth about the whole matter. I miss you so much, *ma chérie,* and the children miss you, too. I don't know what to do about their baths. They are big girls now, and would be abashed if I should see them bathe. I don't think they can manage the water by themselves.

I love you,
Ed.

On Monday of the following week, Papa received an answer:

Ed:

Don't write to me, and don't call me Angel. I'm not an angel, and never pretended to be. I'm not coming home. You can fix the bath water, and leave the room, to return between each bath to replenish the water. After that perfumed handkerchief I doubt if you will miss me.

Regretfully,

Estelle.

It was a whole week before we could send another letter, because of the mail service. Papa fumed and fretted, getting in our way as we tried to keep house.

Margaret swept the floors, sweeping the dirt under the rugs to avoid using the dustpan. Papa helped me with the cooking. He didn't cook anything very good, though, in spite of the fact that he was a fine French cook. We had mostly boiled salmon bellies, from the barrel in the storeroom. I had to soak the bellies in cold water for twenty-four hours before I boiled them because they were so salty. I also boiled some of the salted beef that Mamma had in another barrel. Sometimes I boiled potatoes with the bellies or the beef. They didn't taste just right, so Margaret, Thalia, and Noel refused to eat them. They filled up on whipped cream, which I loved to make and served regularly on huge slices of bread.

I had another letter ready on Monday:

Dear Sweet,

Nothing seems the same with you away. I miss the faint perfume of your hair, the soft touch of your velvet hand. I long to kiss you, *ma chérie;* to press you to my breast.

She didn't put the handkerchief into my pocket. If you'll come home, I'll explain.

Longingly,

Ed.

The *Elmo* carried away Papa's letter, and we settled down for another week of waiting.

On Tuesday, Mr. Stark came to visit.

"Angie," Papa said, "get out your mother's cookbook, and try to bake a cake for Mr. Stark."

"Oh, yes, Papa. I will," I agreed enthusiastically.

I got the cookbook, turned to "cakes," and found a recipe that was quite smeared. "This must be the one Mamma uses," I thought, "because it's so messy all over the page." It was called *Golden Sponge Cake*.

I followed the recipe as it read: "1 cup egg yolks, 2 cups sugar, 2½ cups flour, 2 teaspoonsful baking powder, ½ teaspoon salt, 2 tablespoons butter, ⅞ cup boiling water, lemon extract." I put the ingredients into the bowl, in the exact order as read, only I couldn't find any baking powder, so I used soda. Mamma often put soda in her cakes.

When I poured the boiling water over the other ingredients, it didn't seem just like it did when Mamma baked a cake; it got kind of lumpy, and stuck together in such a way as to make mixing quite difficult.

"Oh, well," I thought, "everything's in the bowl. It'll be all right when it's baked."

The baked cake didn't smell as good as I had expected it to, nor was it in the least spongy, like a well-balanced sponge cake should be. I thought it might improve when I had put the whipped cream on top.

We had pans and pans of cream in the milk room. I wasn't disposed to buttermaking, so we just let the cream collect, hoping Mamma might come any Monday.

I stuck my hand into a pan of milk, and lifted up the whole top. I put the thick cream into a bowl and whipped it stiff. Then I poured about a third of a bottle of vanilla into it, and added plenty of sugar.

"Mamma never gets her whipping cream sweet enough," I said. I piled the delicious mixture over the cake.

Margaret and I cooked an excellent dinner for Mr. Stark. I didn't have time to soak the salmon bellies, but I guessed they'd be all right. "Some people like salt," I told Margaret.

The potatoes were slightly scorched. I put the unburned ones in a fresh kettle, added more water, and reboiled them. They tasted only a *little* burned. Margaret helped me cream the carrots. We poured some thick cream over them and threw in a cup of flour. Margaret thought the cream was a trifle gluey, after the flour was put in.

"Oh, it's fine," I said. "It won't run all over our plates."

We called Papa and Mr. Stark to dinner.

"Well, well," said Mr. Stark to Papa. "What a fine pair of cooks you have."

I didn't think anyone was very enthusiastic over the dinner. Thalia and Noel weren't eating much. Mr. Stark didn't seem to care for his usual two helpings either. But there was still the cake!

It was a beautiful cake. The cream was a soft, yellow shade. I noticed when I cut into its rather lumpy texture that the yellow of the cream blended nicely with the green of the cake. I hadn't known that the soda would have that effect!

Papa took a look at his portion, and then at Mr. Stark. "Suppose we eat our cake outside, like the kids do," he suggested.

"By all means," Mr. Stark answered. "Sometimes cake tastes better when eaten out-of-doors."

Papa and Mr. Stark picked up their cake and walked out the door.

"I don't like this cake," pouted Thalia. "It's got little pieces of egg all over in it."

"Eat your cake and shut up!" I snapped.

"No, I won't," answered Thalia. "I'll be excused, please," and she pushed away from the table.

"The cream is lovely," purred Margaret, blissfully scooping up a large spoonful.

Noel stuck his fingers into the cream and licked them off.

"Won't eat the green cake," he announced.

I bravely tried to swallow another piece of the nasty-tasting, green, lumpy mess; it gagged me. Picking up the cake, I walked out to the pig slop and dumped it in.

"My," said Margaret, "sure'll be some sick pigs tomorrow."

On Monday, Papa got another letter:

Ed:

I'm having a wonderful time. Dances, parties, theater. I feel ten years younger. If you want to smell perfume, press that hussy's handkerchief to your nose. It's still in your pocket.

Estelle.

Another week elapsed; most of our clothes were piled in the wash room. We wore everything for days at a time to conserve.

"I guess I'll have to do the washing," Papa announced. He put the boiler of water on the stove to heat. "We'll put the clothes in and boil them," he said.

Papa went to the fog signal to finish his polishing while the water heated.

Margaret and I gathered up our clothing, together with that of Thalia and Noel. We put them all into the boiler together.

"We'll surprise Papa," I said. "The washing will all be boiled when he comes back."

Papa came in just as the boiler of clothes was bubbling merrily. "What a mess," he roared, lifting the clothes out with a clothes stick. "Ruined, everything ruined—and the baby's woolens are shrunk to nothing! Don't you know better than to put the colored things in with the white? And you never boil woolens."

"No," I answered, "Mamma didn't ever tell me that." "Write another letter to Mamma," ordered Papa. I wrote:

Dear Angel,

I'm glad you're having a good time, but don't you think you should come home?

The children miss you so, and my back itches something awful without you to scratch it. I can't sleep nights.

Please come home.

Ed.

We sent the letter on Monday, and waded through the dust for another week of waiting. Things weren't going so well in the milk room. It smelled rather queer. I suspected that the accumulated cream was spoiling.

"I *should* make the butter," I said, "but I hate to scald out the churn." The churn was a large, barrel-like affair, which was mounted on trunnions. A handle protruded from the side of the barrel. I didn't like to stand still long enough to turn the churn until the cream inside should turn to butter.

On Monday, we had a letter:

Ed:

Rub your back against a tree. I'm staying here.

Estelle.

Things got pretty bad before the next Monday. Noel had a fever and I was worried about him, and Thalia spoke of a headache. We were all at the boathouse when the *Elmo* came in and Mamma got off.

We ran. We shouted and whooped! We were the gladdest kids on earth.

"Oh, Mamma! Mamma!" we all screeched at once. "We've missed you so much!"

Papa held Mamma tight. "Oh, darling! Sweet!" he cried.

Mamma pushed him away. She opened her purse and took out a letter. "I didn't come home because you wanted me to, Ed, although I'm ready to forgive you now. This is what brought me home." She held up a letter.

I read the letter aloud for Papa's benefit:

Deer mamma—

i dont feel so gude Ange dont Kook very gude. i think i will die. plese com hom

i luv you
Thalia.

"I sent it to Mamma," shouted Thalia. "I sent it last Monday. I stamped it and put it in the mail sack all by myself!"

"You're a sweetheart," declared Papa. He picked Thalia up and kissed her.

"Don't! Your mustache tickles," she protested. Mamma looked at Thalia. "My stars!" she exclaimed, "what's that all over your face?" Her eyes also took in Noel's spotted face.

"Measles!"

The days were growing warm and longer. The Alpine lilies were blooming everywhere. The island was fragrant with their perfume. Everywhere were signs that summer was near.

Mamma announced that school was over for the summer, and we were free to roam the island until September. We loved the summer. The big girls and Roy and Lynn always came home, and they took over a lot of the hard work. So we had more time to play. Of course, we all had to work in the gardens. There were four gardens, and the watering had to be done with buckets. Also there was a lot of weeding to spoil an otherwise perfect summer. But, as we all did these chores in a body (even Noel had to help in the garden), we made a game of it and the work wasn't quite so much drudgery.

June arrived, and with the first day of summer came Myra, my cousin from New York, and she knew everything! Myra was beautiful, a blonde girl of thirteen years, who possessed the loveliest curls I had ever seen. She had her curls pulled to the back of her head in grown-up fashion, and they were secured by an enormous hair bow. Her bow had seventeen loops. The largest bow belonging to Clara or Estelle had only ten loops. Myra's covered the entire back of her head.

CHAPTER ELEVEN ︷

And Myra had *slippers*. My older sisters had to wear high-top button shoes with low heels, but Myra had slippers for *everyday* wear and they had *high heels!* Mamma wouldn't let even Clara or Estelle have high heels, except for dancing.

"You're too young," she always said. They were both older than Myra.

When Myra unpacked her trunk, my older sisters and I sat on the bed and watched her. I was fascinated with the pretty underthings. There were exquisite camisoles—that's what Myra called them. I had always heard them referred to as corset covers, but then Myra was from New York, and she knew. And Myra's chemises were silk. I had never seen any silk underthings before; all our things were made from flour sacks, with homemade lace for trimming. But Myra even had 'boughten' lace for the ruffles on her panties. When she walked, she kicked up her heels a little so the boys would see the lace. My older sisters were shocked, and Mamma didn't seem too pleased either.

My sisters didn't like Myra, but I was fascinated by her, and we became fast friends.

As the summer progressed, I acquainted Myra with all the secrets of the island, and she acquainted me with some of the secrets of romance. She had been kissed by *three* different men, she admitted.

Myra told me about the thrills of lovemaking and admonished me not to speak of it to Mamma. I didn't see what harm it would do Mamma though, because I knew that she must know a great deal about love herself. On several occasions I had seen Mamma and Papa holding hands and kissing, down by the water's edge at night. I had sneaked up on them, and had heard Papa tell Mamma that she was still the most beautiful woman in the world, and that he loved her better than ever. Yes, I thought, Mamma must know about love; but Myra warned me to be silent, so I didn't tell.

Myra gave me a book that had been hidden in the bottom of her trunk. The book was called *Hearts Aflame,* and was all about a girl named Frenchy who was in love with a married man. It was an enchanting book. I had never been allowed to read anything but the best children's books that came in the lighthouse circulating library. Mamma went through the library each time it was renewed, and picked out all the books she didn't think were fit for children. So I didn't know a single thing about love affairs.

Myra warned me to hide *Hearts Aflame* so Mamma wouldn't find it. She said, "Your Mamma's too innocent for that sort of book; she wouldn't approve of it. She might even make you burn it up."

I didn't want to do anything to make Mamma less innocent, so I carefully hid the book in the same tree where Millie, my mouse, had her nest. When Millie chewed a hole in the book, ruining some of the best love words, I put it in a tobacco can, to protect it against further damage. Many pleasant afternoons I had, hidden away in a cave overlooking the sea and reading about Frenchy.

"Oh, crush me to your heart, until our passion is spent!" begged Frenchy of her lover Armand.

I didn't know what "passion" was so I looked it up in the large dictionary, and it said it was "an enduring of inflicted pain." I wondered why Frenchy should be wanting pain. Myra told me that love was a thrilling pleasure. I wanted to ask Mamma about these things, but I was afraid to let her be harmed by the book.

Myra taught me to walk like city ladies. She said that the way I walked, with a hop-skip-and-jump, was very unladylike, and that she would be ashamed to have her friends in the city see me walk. So she set about teaching me to walk correctly. First, she made me stick the sitting down part of me far out in back; then my chest must be thrust far out in front. I was then supposed to hold my legs tight together, and take tiny little steps. It was a strained and uncomfortable position for walking; my back ached terribly after each lesson. I finally mastered the art to Myra's complete satisfaction.

One day I was practicing my peculiar walk, when Mamma called to me to come into the house. "Angie," she asked, "what on earth causes you to stick yourself out in that outlandish fashion? From the way you were walking, and the manner in which you hold your legs, one would judge that you were in distress."

"I'm walking like a city lady, Mamma," I answered. "Myra is teaching me so I can visit her in New York some day."

Mamma laughed. "Well, you may as well quit right now. For one thing, you are never going to visit Myra in the city, if I can prevent it; for another, if I ever catch you walking like that again, I'll switch the skin off your legs. No lady, city or otherwise, walks that way."

I knew that Mamma meant what she said, and anyway I was pleased to resume my comfortable hop-skip-and-jump walk.

When Myra went home the following Monday, Mamma, Estelle, and Clara were glad to see her go. I was sad; I knew I should miss Myra a lot—she had given me so much to think about. She had awakened in me a curiosity about life. From Myra I had learned that where boys were concerned my future held many surprises.

The Patos Island boathouse where Angie unexpectedly launched her two day voyage.
Photo courtesy of the National Archives, Pacific Alaska Region (Seattle)

CHAPTER TWELVE

I t was pleasant in the old crooked tree. My back was supported by its forked trunk. I was almost asleep.

"Angie," I heard someone say, "Angie, go to the boathouse. Go to the boathouse, Angie."

I leaned over and looked at the door of the house. "Who's down there?" I asked. No one answered.

In my mind, I heard the words again. "Go to the boathouse."

"I will go to the boathouse," I said to myself. "I was wanting to go there, anyway."

Climbing down from the tree, I set out for the boathouse, walking slowly and stopping to play with everything I met along the way. An old hen with some tiny black chickens was scratching in the barnyard for maggots. I turned over a few cow dungs for her and laughed to see her little chickens scamper in for the feast.

Picking up a stick, I drew it smartly all the way across the pickets of the goose pen. I loved to hear the gander squawk in rage. I swung for a minute or two on a cedar bough. A little further along the way, near the rock pile, I hesitated to see if any new snakes had been born. Little snakes are so cute. I didn't find any, so I walked on.

Finally, I was near the boathouse. Hearing Bully bellowing, down at the Head-of-the-Bay, I looked to see what he was doing. Then I heard the voice again.

"Angie—Angie!"

I looked in the direction of the sound, and there was Mamma.

She was standing on a rock, halfway between Patos and Little Patos. Bully was standing facing her from the shore; he was in a rage. I ran a short distance down the bank, and yelled to Mamma.

"I'll get Papa."

She waved to me that she understood, and I ran toward home. Papa was in the fog signal.

"Come quickly, Papa," I cried. "Bully has Mamma in the water!"

Papa hurried to the barn, where he armed himself with a pitchfork. Then, seeing Bill standing by in the orchard, he mounted the surprised horse and slapped him into a run. Guiding him by his halter, he set off for the Head-of-the-Bay. I stood on the hill by the boathouse and watched.

Papa reached Bully, and began spearing at him with the pitchfork. Bully ran away. Then Papa helped Mamma in from the dangerous rock. She was soaking wet, and sick with fear. Papa made her walk fast all the way home so she wouldn't catch cold.

"He followed me to the beach," explained Mamma, "right to the water's edge. Ed, you'll have to get rid of that bull; he'll kill some of us yet!"

At home, I said, "Lucky for you I was at the boathouse, Mamma."

Mamma looked at me, then. "Angie," she said, "why were you at the boathouse?"

"I heard a voice," I answered. "The voice said, 'Angie, go to the boathouse.'"

"That's queer." Mamma's face had a strange expression on it. "When I was calling for help, I could have almost sworn that I saw an old gray-haired man standing on the rocks behind the boathouse."

I gulped and didn't answer Mamma. "Could she have seen God?" I wondered.

"Curly! Curly," I called, one morning. Curly didn't come bounding after me as he usually did. "That's funny," I said. "He always comes." I went in search of the dog.

I found Curly lying in a corner of the barn; he didn't get up when I approached. Instead he groaned and retched.

"He's sick," I said. "I'll get Al."

At my summons Al hastened to the barn and knelt beside the stricken dog.

"Been eating rotten salmon," he said. "He's poisoned!" Returning to the house, Al melted a cup of lard; he took it to the barn and poured it down Curly's throat.

"Will he get well, now?" I asked anxiously.

"I hope it will do him some good," said Al. "Dogs don't usually recover from salmon poisoning, though." He brought Curly some bread that had been soaked in milk, and forced the dog to swallow a small amount. "We'll leave him alone for a while. He may recover, and he may not."

For several days, Curly hovered between life and death. Mary and Al worked over him patiently. Then, on the sixth day, Curly disappeared.

"He's gone away to die." Al had tears in his eyes; his voice was weak and quavery.

"How do you know?" I asked.

"It's always the way, Angel. Dogs crawl away and hide when they're ready to die."

"I'll hunt for him," I answered. I went to the prayer tree. "God, God, where is Curly hiding?" I asked.

"Don't ask that question, Angel." God spoke softly. "Curly wouldn't want to be spied upon."

"Save him!" I said.

"No, Angel, you must not command God." He was angry now.

I jumped up and walked away. "I'll find him," I said. But I didn't find Curly. After two weeks he showed up at my prie-dieu one morning. I had just knelt to pray when he got up from the dark hole he was lying in and licked my hand.

"Oh, Curly, Curly," I cried, "you didn't die!"

"No," said God. "He merely buried himself in the swamp and the mud drew out the poison. I watched over him while he was there. I couldn't let you know where he was until he was over the worst of it."

I lovingly carried Curly all the way home. "God saved him!" I shouted.

"Well, I'll be damned," swore Papa. "If that dog has survived salmon poisoning, God must have had a hand in it."

Everyone was very happy about Curly's recovery, and petted and pampered him. He recuperated rapidly, and soon was running about again. He wagged his tail for joy when Al, armed with a shotgun, said, "Come on, Curly—ducks."

Christmas had come and gone; the snow lay deep on the island, a silvery carpet spreading over the bare rocks and grassy meadows.

Roy, Clara, Estelle, and Lynn, home for the holidays, were enjoying the winter sports. We skated on the pond, romped in the snow with the smaller children, and took hikes around the island.

Clara enjoyed playing with Thalia, who was a big girl now, and beginning to go about the island; she was happy to have Clara for company. Thalia had received a large, double-jointed doll for Christmas, and to her delight, Clara sewed new dresses for it.

To pass the long evening hours, we played "Flinch," or the game of "Fox and Geese" that Lynn had received for Christmas. This was an interesting game, enjoyed by the whole family. It had checkers and a spinner, and a black fox. The object of the game was to move the geese over the checkerboard in such a manner as to avoid being cornered by the fox.

Papa popped corn on those winter evenings; Mamma brought apples from the cellar, or large plates of ginger cookies. Often we had a taffy pull, and sometimes someone would read aloud a good rollicking story. The evenings passed quickly—too quickly; we hated to go to bed.

One day, during the holidays, Clara and I were walking around the island near the outside garden when we heard something

CHAPTER TWELVE ∿

crashing in the brush. Almost immediately we saw Bully emerge from the woods ahead of us, to come trotting up the path in our direction.

"Quick! Quick! Under the fence!" Clara gasped, and we began to run. From inside the garden fence, we stood watching as Bully thundered by on the path. He saw us as he rushed by, then whirled and started back.

"Let's cross the garden to the beach side," said Clara. "We can roll under the wire and reach the bluff before Bully notices that we're out. Then we'll go home by way of the rocks." When halfway across the garden, we realized that we had underestimated the thinking capacity of Bully.

He was also approaching the other side of the garden. When we reached the point of our intended exit, Bully was waiting for us, and was already butting at the wire fence.

On the same side of the garden, Papa had built a stile with steep steps and a wide platform at the top.

"Let's sit down on the stile until he goes away," I suggested.

We brushed the snow from the platform and settled ourselves for a long wait. We watched the angry bull as he pawed the ground and bellowed, intermittently bumping the fence and fir trees. We called, shouted, and whistled, hoping someone would wander near enough to hear us, or that Curly might come to our rescue.

Bully, tired of butting trees, had approached the stile. He looked the steps over, as if contemplating climbing them. Both Clara and I began to exercise our vocal cords, singly and in unison.

"Look," exclaimed Clara excitedly, pointing to the woods near the path.

I looked. There, in the path directly facing Bully and in full view, was God.

"It's God!" I joyfully screamed. "Oh, God, help us—help us!"
Clara stood speechless.

God raised his arms and waved both of them at the bull. Bully lowered his head and charged. God disappeared into the brush.

"Come on, let's run for the bluff," said Clara. We fairly flew through the salal brush to reach the bluff. Sliding over, we dropped to the rocks beneath. We were safe.

Bully was roaring and bellowing far behind us, before we stopped for breath. Then Clara said, "Who was that old man?"

"God," I answered.

"Oh, don't be silly."

"It is God," I answered. "It's the same God I told Mamma about, long ago—only no one believes me."

"I'm going to tell Papa about him," said Clara. "He'll find him and send him away."

"Oh, please, please don't," I begged. I told her all about how God had saved me when I was adrift at sea; of all my promises to Him.

Clara was silent for a long time. Then she spoke, "All right, I won't say anything; I'm not sure just what to do about it, though. God couldn't be a man. He's not a material person; He's Divine—no one has ever seen Him, and no one ever will."

"That's not so," I answered. "God is sometimes revealed to those who believe in Him, and are pure in heart—*For they shall see God.*"

"Well," said Clara, "*you're* not pure in heart, and you can believe anything you want to about that old man. I won't tell Papa about him, if you will promise not to run about the island alone; he might harm you."

"No," I replied, "he won't hurt me, and I won't promise, but I think you're ungrateful to God for saving you from Bully today; and if you tell Papa about God—I'll—I'll tell Mama about Dick Blane squeezing you and kissing you on the beach every time he comes."

"Oh, shut up," answered Clara.

We walked home in silence. Clara told Papa about Bully keeping us marooned on the stile, but never once did she mention God.

The *Elmo* had just been there and gone, and Mamma was reading her mail. There was a letter from Estelle. Mamma read it out loud:

Dear Mamma,

I'll be home on the *Elmo* next Monday.

Guess what? I'm bringing a young man home with me. He's my beau, Mamma, and please be nice to him. I like him a lot and he likes me. His name is Criss Waters, and Mamma, he's divine.

Oh, I almost forgot—when Criss comes, I don't want Angie to talk to him. She might tell him about her "voices" and I don't want Criss to think I have a crazy sister. Mamma, will you please, talk to her about it.

Affectionately, your daughter,
Estelle.

I was pretty burned up about that letter.

"Hell-damn!" I swore. I was so mad that I didn't even feel the slap that Mamma gave me. "I'm not crazy. Well, I'll show her—I won't even be nice to her old beau; I won't even speak to him; and what's more, I won't even give up my bedroom for him."

I stormed out, knowing that I'd have to give up my room. It was the only room that could be converted to a guest room. I determined to snub Estelle and her Criss, however.

When Monday and the *Elmo* arrived, I didn't go to the boat-house with the rest. I ran away by myself. Climbing a tree that commanded a clear view of the landing, I settled down to wait. Clara, Estelle, Lynn, and Roy climbed out of the small boat, and then I saw Criss. He was a handsome boy. I almost lost my balance—almost forgot my determination to snub him. Why, Criss was the best-looking boy I'd ever seen.

I climbed down from the tree and ran all the way home. Hurrying to my room, which was made up for the guest, I reached under the covers and withdrew "Puffy," the toad.

"Some other time," I whispered to him.

I had tidied my hair, hastily put on shoes and stockings, and dabbed a bit of Mamma's perfume on the front of my dress before the family and Criss reached the house. Mamma introduced me to Criss and, instead of saying "Hello" and ducking my head, as I usually did when introduced, I stammered "How do you do?" and extended my hand.

Estelle stared at me, and then a gleam entered her eye. "Mamma," she said, "hadn't Angela better go out and play with her dolls?"

"Dolls?" I yelled. "You know perfectly well I haven't played with dolls since I was a little girl."

"Well, you're only twelve, now," victoriously answered Estelle.

The war was on.

Estelle kept Criss away from me pretty well, but I persevered and one day I saw my chance. Estelle was shampooing her hair. It was quite a chore to shampoo Estelle's hair—it was thick and long—and Mamma had to help her. It would take at least two hours before the hair would be dry.

I found Criss down by the boathouse. He was just sitting on a log, whistling and looking out over the water. I sat down beside him.

"You're the best-looking man I've ever seen," I said.

He turned and smiled at me. "Go on, you must have kissed the Blarney stone."

"What's the Blarney stone?" I asked, moving closer.

"It's a stone in Blarney Castle, Ireland," he answered. "When you kiss it, you can talk sweet words."

"Are you from Ireland, and have you ever kissed the Blarney stone?" I asked.

"Hey, not so fast! One at a time," he said. "First, I am Irish, but I've never kissed the stone. I wish I had, though, because then I'd have the courage to talk to your sister. I can't say the things I want to."

Just then Millie, my mouse, ran past. Criss jumped up and threw a stick at her.

"Oh, don't," I said. "That's Millie—she's my pet; she talks to me."

Criss looked at me in amazement. "A pet mouse that talks?" he asked.

The secret was out—now he'd think I was crazy. I hung my head and stammered, "No—yes—she doesn't really *talk,* but she says things to me."

Criss laughed. He took my hand in his and we both sat down again.

"Maybe she's a leprechaun," he said. I listened while he told me about leprechauns, the little people of Ireland's folklore tales. When he had finished, I jumped up and clapped my hands.

"Oh, Criss!" I said. "You're just like me—you believe just like I do." Then I told him all about the voices and the face in the woods—the years of shame—how I found God, and how everyone called me "psychic." I finished with Estelle's letter and the remark about being crazy.

Criss looked me straight in the eye. "You're on the right track, sister."

"Am I going to be your sister?" I asked.

He looked thoughtful. "I'd ask Estelle to marry me, but I don't know the right words. When I'm with her, I can't think of anything to say."

"Oh, I'll teach you," I volunteered. "I know all the love words."

I stood up, faced Criss squarely, and began. "Oh, my love, at last we are alone. Alone, and now I must crush you to my heart. Your lips are hot on mine, darling. Our passion—"

"Stop!" yelled Criss. With a twinkle in his blue eyes, he asked, "Angie, are you making love to me?" I opened my mouth in amazement, the hot blood rushing to my cheeks. I started to run.

Criss caught me. "Come back, Angel," he said. "I want to know where you learned those love words. Perhaps I can get some help."

I ran to the hole in the Mouse Tree and brought back the book *Hearts Aflame.*

"Look," I said. "They're all here in this wonderful book—only Millie chewed it some—she wanted the paper for her nest."

Criss took the book, thumbed through it for a few minutes.

"Where did you get this trash?" he asked. "No wonder Millie wanted the paper for her nest. This book is hot stuff. Angel, you must throw *Hearts Aflame* overboard right now while I'm watching. I don't want my little sister reading such trash."

I duly tore *Hearts Aflame* in several pieces and threw it into the sea.

"Am I going to be your little sister?"

"I hope so," he answered.

We were halfway home when we met Estelle. Her freshly shampooed hair shone like satin. She cast an accusing look at me.

"Angie, Mamma wants you," she said.

"I'm sure going to have a fine little sister," said Criss. Estelle was astonished. "Sister?"

"Yes," answered Criss. "My new little sister-in-law."

"Oh, Criss, I've hoped you'd ask me," wept Estelle.

"I've wanted to, all along," said Criss, "but I couldn't until Angel taught me the words."

"Oh, Criss, isn't Angel precious?" bubbled Estelle.

Summertime came lazily drifting in, trailing its garments of brightly hued flowers, to settle itself on the island.

The young people were home again for the vacation months. This time, Clara brought Bill Oldenburg with her for a week's visit. Bill was a handsome young man whom Clara had met at a party. The two had been "going together" now for several months. We liked Bill from the moment we first saw him. He had a winning smile and a courteous manner.

I began to fix myself up, as I now did on every occasion of a visiting male.

"It's no use, Angel," said Mary. "Don't singe your wings against a flame. Bill is your sister's beau. You're still a little girl, and your prince is on his way."

"Pooh," I answered. "I'm not fixing up for Bill." But I knew in my heart that I *was,* and I hung around him whenever I could.

Before the week was out, Clara announced that she and Bill were to be married. I forgot my pretended love in the joyful anticipation of a wedding for Clara.

Oh, the happy, busy days that preceded Clara's wedding. They were to be married in August, and Mamma and Mary helped Clara with her sewing. They made lacy underthings, petticoats, and dresses, and an organdy wedding gown. Mamma and the girls made innumerable trips to Bellingham to shop. There were bridesmaids' gowns and finery of all sorts on Mamma's list.

Invitations to the wedding were dispatched to everyone we knew, both in the cities and on the surrounding islands. It was to be a grand affair.

Time sped by; there were only two days left before the wedding day. Al bought new dance music for his Victrola, and a record of Lohengrin's wedding march. Papa brought wax to make the veranda smooth for dancing. Mamma and we girls spent our time cooking and baking for the wedding feast. Mamma baked a three-tiered silver cake, which she frosted in white with a scalloped edging of pale yellows. When our baking was finished, there were numerous cakes, nut breads, French pastries, Swedish cookies, and loaves of white bread. Then Mamma began to roast the geese, turkeys, hens, pork, and beef.

"You have food enough for a regiment," remarked Papa.

"We don't have a wedding every day," Mamma replied, "and many of our guests from Bellingham and Seattle will be staying over."

Papa and Al built a long table under the trees, and on the day of the wedding Mamma laid three white banquet cloths over it. On each end of the table we placed a silver basket of roses and white carnations.

The guests had been arriving since early morning. They came in launches, sloops, fishing boats, and a chartered steamer from Bellingham. When they were all present, I counted seventy-five guests, not including Bill's family and the minister.

The wedding was held on the veranda, where Al and Mary had built an arch of white carnations.

Al started his Victrola; the strains of the wedding march floated out on the air. Estelle, dressed in a long blue lace dress, approached the altar. In a moment, Clara came slowly walking through the door on Papa's arm, to the altar, and joined hands with Bill while the service was read. Clara and Bill repeated their vows, and were pronounced man and wife. . . .

When the ceremony was over, the guests all gathered around for the refreshments. I was more interested in the banquet than I was in the wedding. So I disappeared immediately, but not before I saw Lynn put a record on the Victrola. From the yard, I heard the blatant tones of "There'll Be a Hot Time in the Old Town Tonight."

Mamma was fixing the coffee things for serving, so she could vouch for me if I should be accused of playing the record. I sighed with relief, and began to contemplate the large ice-cream freezers.

The feast and the dancing were over. The wedding gifts had all been viewed, and a general movement toward the boathouse began. Some of the guests had a long trip by water ahead of them.

Clara was helping to entertain those who remained, when a young man stepped up to her.

"Bill's waiting on my boat, the *Cricket*," he said. "Slip out and join us, and we'll be off to Bellingham."

Clara hastily made her way to her room, gathered up her luggage and, unseen by the reveling guests, went to the boathouse. She was put aboard the *Cricket* at once, and it immediately put out to sea.

Bill appeared from nowhere. "Where's Clara?" he asked me.

Before I could answer, a young man stepped between us. "She's waiting on my boat, the *Morning Star*. We'll join her there. Hurry, before you're noticed."

I began to protest; then, changing my mind, I put my hand over my mouth. Bill followed the young man to the *Morning Star*, quickly boarded her, and the boat moved away in the direction of Friday Harbor.

Bill was off on his honeymoon, going in the opposite direction from Clara, his bride! I knew that it would be two days before Bill could catch the *Chippewa* and meet Clara in Bellingham!

Semiahmoo Lighthouse, circa 1915, where Helene's father served as head keeper after leaving Patos Island. *Photo courtesy of Coast Guard Museum Northwest*

CHAPTER THIRTEEN

In November, Lynn was the only one who returned for the Thanksgiving holidays. Estelle and Roy couldn't leave their jobs.

"Our family is breaking up," mourned Papa.

"As all families do," answered Mamma. "You can't keep them together forever."

"In the city we could have kept them longer," said Papa. "How much longer are you going to keep me prisoner on this devilish island? It got René, Edmund, Elizabeth, and Laurel. I tell you it's breaking up our family. There's an evilness about Patos. I had bad luck when we lived here before. I want to get off. I still believe I can find Spanish John."

"Don't blame Patos for our troubles," said Mamma. "The island has been a blessing to us. Any adversity was caused by our own stupidity. We'll stay until our job is finished."

Papa muttered something under his breath, and, turning, stalked out of the house.

"What did he say?" asked Mamma.

"He said 'devilish island,'" I answered.

That night it rained. I slept restlessly. Toward morning I was awakened by voices coming from Mamma's room.

"All the guns. Every one—and bring as much ammunition as you can carry. There's no time to waste. Wear something dark, so you'll be inconspicuous."

I slipped out of bed and pulled my overalls on over my nightgown. Papa's words frightened me. I guessed from past experiences that we were going to have unwelcome visitors. Tiptoeing to Lynn's room, I called guardedly, "Lynn, Lynn."

He didn't answer, and when I reached his bed I discovered he was gone.

It was then I heard the dull pounding of a motor. I stepped to the window and looked out. There was a large boat running without lights, and heading straight for the lighthouse.

"Pirates—or smugglers!"

"Angie, get back into bed," ordered Mamma from the hallway.

Then I heard guns.

Al came running to the porch. "They're being chased!" he shouted. "There's another boat coming in from behind Little Patos."

"God!" said Papa. "What a night for murder." He turned to Mamma and Al. "You're the soldier, Al. You'd better take command."

"You go to the station," said Al. "Lynn and I will follow by way of the rocks. Keep hidden until they force us out. They may go past—I hope. Keep out of sight."

Mary ran to Al's side. "Where do I go?" she asked.

"You stay in the house, but watch from the window. They may attack us here. Take the .45."

"Be careful," Mary warned. She ran back indoors. I disobeyed Mamma and quietly followed at a distance when she went to the fog signal.

The rain beat against my face. The night was quite dark, but the two boats loomed large and black as they approached the island.

I reached the shelter of the fog signal. I saw Papa and Mamma inside; I slipped in and stood behind one of the engines.

"Here," whispered Papa. "Put them in here." Mamma carried the guns to the engine room, and arranged each one in a convenient position for quick use.

"They're heading for the point," she said. "They'll run aground in this low tide."

"Hell," answered Papa. "The light's working. It's a poor mariner who'd run aground right under the nose of the lighthouse."

"They aren't mariners. They're smugglers, and running for their lives," reminded Mamma.

There were more shots as pursued and pursuer neared the point.

Papa stepped outside. "Hell," he shouted, "they *are* going to run aground; they're too close in." He ran to the rocky point and climbed down near the water.

Mamma went outside, carrying a rifle. I followed close behind. She noticed me then. "Go to the house!" she hissed.

"I'm afraid," I answered. "I'll stay close to you. Please let me stay with you."

"I guess you'll have to," she snapped. "There's no time for taking you back now. Stay close behind me!"

The night was cold and clammy. I began to be sorry I hadn't stayed in bed.

"Crash-boo-o-oomm!" The fleeing boat struck head on against the reef.

"God-damn!" said Papa. "That was deliberate. They intentionally ran aground. Get the red lantern!"

Mamma and I hurried back to the fog signal for a red lantern. We fairly flew back to Papa's side.

"Follow me, and keep me covered!" Papa yelled to Lynn and Al, who had crept into sight around the edge of the bluff. Curly followed close at Al's heels.

Papa flung the red lantern from left to right, running and shouting, "Keep away! Keep away!" Then, reaching the spit, he whirled the red light in circles around his head. "Danger! Danger!" he shouted.

The pursuing craft slowed and swung out. We could hear her rudder squeak loudly as she changed her course. The shooting stopped. There was not a word from those on board, and no one was visible on deck.

The long, unlighted boat cleared the reef and swung down the island toward Blanchard's Harbor.

Papa and Al held a consultation.

"Now what?" asked Papa.

"We're bound to go to the rescue of those aboard the stranded boat," answered Al. "That's our duty. What do you advise?"

"There doesn't seem to be any sign of life aboard her," said Papa. "I advise careful movement on our part. Lynn, run up to the tower. Crouch down behind the railing on the observation deck and watch that pirate. Tell me if she stops or goes on to Blanchard's Harbor. Damn Blanchard's Harbor! It's the hideout for every damn smuggler between Port Townsend and Japan."

"The cutter won't be back for two days," advised Al. "They're changing shifts."

"Yes," answered Papa, "we'll probably all be murdered. Why couldn't this have happened yesterday, when the revenue cutter was here?"

I shivered, and wondered if dying would be very dreadful, but I didn't cry. I stooped down and patted Curly. "We're not afraid, are we?" I asked him. I began to quake with fear. Curly licked my nose.

Papa waded out to within hailing distance of the stranded boat.

"Hello!" he boomed. There was no answer.

"Bring my megaphone, Angie," Papa ordered. I ran to the fog signal and hurried back with the megaphone. Papa raised it to his mouth.

"Hello on board!" he shouted again.

In a moment a voice answered. "G'wan away and mind your business!"

"The hell I will," shouted Papa. "Get out of there and come ashore!"

"Come and get me!" taunted the voice.

Then another voice shouted, "We're wounded—we need help!"

"Shut up!" roared the first voice. There was a sound of scuffling within the cabin. Then the first voice spoke again.

"Just you leave us be, Captain. We'll float off this reef and be gone at high tide."

Papa roared again. "You'll be damned! There's a hole in your boat as big as a man's head. And high tide will never float you. You're above high tide mark!"

The voices were silent.

Lynn came scurrying to Papa's side. "They stopped down by the spring, and they're coming ashore in their skiff."

"I was afraid of that," said Al. "This fellow on the reef must have a valuable cargo. He doesn't want us prying, and the hijacker doesn't want to give up. We're in for a fight."

"There are too many against us," said Mamma. "Don't you think we'd better go to the house and lock ourselves in? They'll fight it out with each other and go away."

"What a hell of a lighthouse keeper you turned out to be," said Papa. "I'd rather lose my life in the line of duty than turn heel to a low-down gang of smugglers. I'm hired here to protect the weak and enforce the law!"

"I'm with you!" said Al. "Get all the extra rope and wire we have available. We may have some tying to do."

"I'm sorry," said Mamma.

"You'd better take the children to safety," said Papa.

"I'll do nothing of the sort." Mamma was indignant. "I'm a good shot and so is Lynn. Lynn, run up to the house and get Mary. Tell her to hurry. The little ones will be all right; I don't believe the men will go near the house."

Lynn ran after Mary. I shivered again, but I didn't want to leave Mamma. I would have liked to take Curly and run to the shelter of the barn.

Mamma said, "Stay close, Angie."

"I'm not afraid," I lied, but I made sure that Curly stayed close behind me. Mary and Lynn came running from the house.

Al took over. "They'll come from the rocks, or over the ridge, or down the path from the house. From any direction they can be seen from the tower. Lynn, go back there and keep us posted. Ed, you take position between the fog signal and the stranded boat. Mary, you hide behind the oil house and watch the path. Mother will watch the ridge, and I'll be everywhere. Keep out of sight and near the ground." Al disappeared, and the others took their posts.

The rain stopped and the night was less dark, but I kept on shivering where I stood with Mamma.

Curly growled and began to bark. I don't know what happened next—everything went so quickly.

Lynn was running all around and saying, "Over there; there's seven of 'em. They're all around us—god damn—god damn—god damn!"

I fell flat on my face on the ground and screamed, "Oh, God, make 'em stop!" Guns began to go off all around me.

I don't know how long I lay in the wet grass, but I aroused myself to hear Curly snarling and snapping very near me, and to see two figures rolling on the ground. The early morning light showed that one of the figures was Al. I jumped to my feet. The two men brushed against me. Then my senses returned. I looked around for Mamma. I couldn't utter a sound—my vocal cords were frozen.

Mamma was standing by the fog signal. She was pointing her revolver at three men who stood against the wall. Lynn was tying a fourth. I stood without moving, and watched. Then Al and the man he was fighting began to roll toward the bank. The man was beating Al over the face. Curly was tearing at the hijacker's shoulders and arms.

"Stop!" I yelled. Stooping down, I picked up a good-sized granite rock and with both hands brought it down on the man's head. He grunted and rolled over.

Al stood up. "Thanks, Angie," he said. His mouth was covered with blood, and his clothes were torn away.

"Curly helped too," I said.

Al didn't stop to chat; he took his ragged shirt and bound the man's hands behind his back.

"He's dead—I killed him," I said. I was too shocked to be excited or sorry. I stared at the blood for a moment; then I was sick to my stomach.

"He might come back to life," said Al. He ran to the oil house. "Mary," he called.

"Here, Al," she answered. "Careful—he has a gun."

Al rounded the flagpole and grappled with the man who held Mary at gun's point. They fell to the ground together.

"Kill 'im with a rock!" I screamed at Mary. From behind the fog signal, someone dashed past me, striking me a nasty blow in the stomach. I doubled up and began to retch. Papa stepped over me and gave chase to the fleeing hijacker.

"Oh—oh—oh," I groaned. My upset stomach felt as if it was coming out of my throat along with its contents.

Sick as I was, I stood up and started after Papa. "Come on, Curly, we hafta help Papa!"

Contrary to custom, Curly didn't follow at my heels. He shot past me and down the path like a rocket, also passing Papa. I caught up to Papa, who was wheezing and blowing as he lumbered up the path in pursuit.

"Angie, go back!"

"No, I hafta catch Curly before the man kills him!" I shouted. I doubled my speed.

I had rolled under the fence, and was on the downhill road to the spring when it happened. From out of the bushes, God appeared. He stood in the path, facing the approaching man. The man stopped short. Throwing up his hands, he shrieked. "John! You."

God spoke not a word. His huge hands grasped the man's head and twisted the face around to the back. I could hear the bones in the neck snap. Then he released his hold, letting the body fall to the ground. Curly growled and sniffed at the man on the ground. God fled noiselessly to the woods.

I looked down at the man, who was lying very still. "That'll teach you not to call God 'John,'" I said. "You should have studied your

Bible better. John was only a servant of God."

Papa caught up to me. "What happened?" he asked.

I braved Papa's displeasure whenever I mentioned God and answered, "God broke his neck because he called him names."

"Angela!" shouted Papa. "I should think you'd tell the truth at a time like this." He slapped my mouth. "This will teach you not to lie." He leaned over the fallen man. "He's dead; I guess he stumbled on this root in the path and twisted his neck when he fell."

After what Papa had done to me, I couldn't very well mention God again. "Maybe I *was* seeing things," I thought.

Papa stood over the dead man a moment. Then he spoke.

"Let's go back and help. This one is out of the fight for good."

I climbed up the path, and glanced out to sea. "Papa," I yelled, "the hijackers' boat is drifting away. It's far out—and so is their skiff."

Papa looked. "Who could have set them adrift?" he wondered.

I was about to answer, "God must have done it," but, remembering the slap, I kept my mouth shut.

Back at the fog signal, Papa asked, "Are they all accounted for?"

"Every one," answered Al. "This was our lucky night. We had the advantage of having had places to hide, and we've caught them all."

Papa looked the scowling men over. "Anybody want to fight?" he asked. No one answered.

"We'd better take them to the house," advised Mamma. "Some of them are in need of medical care."

"What about the boat on the reef?" asked Al. "There are wounded men there, too."

"They'll keep for an hour or so," answered Papa. "We have these men to care for. I guess there's only been one casualty. He's up the trail with a broken neck."

"You killed my brother?" asked a little pickle-faced hijacker.

"No, I didn't kill him," replied Papa. "He tripped over a root in the path—his neck is broken." Then Papa spoke softly to Pickle-Face.

"I'm sorry—but you should have thought about death before you engaged in this dirty business."

"It was none of ya business!" snapped a red-faced mountain of a man. "Why d'n't'cha keep your nose outa it—we wouldn'ta troubled ya none—we was after that low-down smuggler. We didn't aim ta fight ya—ya forced us ta our guns. We ain't got but two weapons among tha lot of us—ya yaller-bellied, snoopin' light tender. Thet guy on tha rocks got a full load o' opium aboard."

"I suppose you weren't intending to hijack the cargo." Mamma's voice was frigid—she looked like a fighting eagle.

"It's none o' ya damned business," snarled the ugly man.

"Shut up!" commanded Al. He jerked the man to his feet and kicked his pants. "Mind your manners around my mother."

The other four hijackers were silent during the walk to the house.

"I thought there were seven men," said Papa. "Lynn, didn't you see seven men coming down the path?"

"I thought I did," answered Lynn. "Maybe there were only six. It was quite dark."

"Lynn and I will stay here and watch," Papa said, "just in case someone else wants to fight. Hurry back, Al. We have business out in front with this shipwreck on the rocks."

I watched the faces of the five men as Al marched them to the house. The pickle-faced man was crying. Large tears ran down his face. I felt sorry for him.

"God really was the one who killed your brother," I told him.

"Shut up, brat—shut up—" wailed Pickle-Face.

"But I have to *tell* someone," I insisted. "He called God 'John.'"

"John?" asked Pickle-Face. He was going to say more but one of the other hijackers motioned him to silence.

The other men looked terribly ugly at me, so I scampered on ahead of the procession. I reached the back entrance hall and was just ready to push open the kitchen door when Curly growled menacingly.

"Whatsa matter?" I asked.

The hair on Curly's neck rose, and he growled again.

I backed out the door. Mamma came up behind me.

"Sh-h-h," I said. "Someone's in there."

Mamma cocked her revolver and stepped inside the entrance. "Who's in there?" she called.

"Nobody; come on in," answered a deep voice.

Just then, Mary and Al came up behind Mamma.

"I'll go around front and surprise him," said Mamma. She crept in through the front door and cautiously entered the kitchen.

"Put down your gun," said the voice. "I'm only eating a piece of this scrumptious pie. I was hungry and helped myself."

There, seated at the kitchen table, sat the seventh of the hijackers.

"How did you get here?" asked Mamma. Al and Mary walked into the kitchen.

"Well, I was watching the boat, an' I decided to do a little looting on my own. After I peeked at the battle and saw we were losing, I decided to get a full belly before getting caught—only I didn't intend to stay so long. An' now, I'll get going—" he whipped out a revolver and pointed it at Al and Mamma. "If you'll kindly get out of my way, I'll be off—"

"No, you don't!" shouted Al, springing straight into the face of the gun. The hijacker was knocked off balance. Mamma shoved the broomstick between his legs and he fell; the gun went off with a bang.

"What's going on?" yelled Papa, dashing into the room.

"Oh, this little boy is just misbehaving," said Al. "He figured to run to the boat and get away."

"You'd better give up, sonny," advised Papa. "You'll find your boat has drifted out into the strait and is several miles away; and, besides, I want you for a guest until the revenue cutter returns—gets real lonesome here sometimes."

The hijackers were ushered into the kitchen. Papa and Al made sure their hands were securely tied. Mary moved chairs from the dining room into the kitchen. The six men were seated in a row.

"My goodness, you all look like devils out of hell in Pilgrim's Progress," I ventured.

"Angie, go to your room!" ordered Mamma.

I went into the hallway and stood peeking through a crack in the door. Mamma and Mary filled the washbasin with hot water, and began to wash and bandage the wounded, scowling men.

Papa opened his shirt. "Here, bandage my shoulder first," he said. "Quite a nasty little nip. I have to hurry back and relieve Lynn. I left him guarding the shipwreck."

"A slug passed through my right calf," Al said, ripping off his trouser leg. "It didn't get a muscle, though."

Mamma stopped helping the hijackers, and bandaged Papa's shoulder and Al's leg. When she had finished, they left for the fog signal. I was torn between a desire to follow the men and a wish to watch Mamma and Mary. I decided to watch for a moment or two, and then to go in search of further excitement. I was thoroughly enjoying myself. All my sickness and fear had vanished.

One of the hijackers had a broken arm; another a broken nose. A third had a sprained wrist. I noticed the awful bruise on the head of a fourth, and realized with some shock and a little horror that he was the man I had "killed" with a rock. The other two were not injured.

"What a mess," I whispered to myself. I slipped out the front door and soon was watching Papa and Al while they put ashore the crew of the stranded launch.

The three men from the launch were wounded. One had a broken leg—he lay on the walk and groaned. Another had a fractured hand, almost shot away, and the third—a boy—had been shot through the abdomen.

"I don't think he'll pull through," said Al.

Papa returned to the launch. He brought ashore her lines and secured them around an iron post that had been placed in the rocks for the sole purpose of anchoring stranded boats.

"It *is* opium," he stated. "A full cargo."

"We're Canadians," spoke the leader of the gang. "Our boat is from Canada; you can't touch us. We ran aground on purpose to get away from that gang of American hijackers."

"You're in American waters, my lad," said Papa, "and we'll hold you for the authorities. You're loaded with opium—and that is my business."

Lynn got the wheelbarrow, and one by one the men were removed to the house.

"The boy is dead!" murmured Mamma, after a hasty examination. Large tears rained down her face. She turned away.

"God, he looks like René!" breathed Papa. His eyes also filled with tears.

I glanced at the dead boy's face. "Oh, he does—he does," I cried.

I ran to my prie-dieu and began to pray, "Oh, God, why'd he hafta die? Why didn't you stop them *before* they killed him?"

I guessed that I never *would* understand God's ways. He had killed the man on the path with his own hands, and had let the boy die.

Two days later when the Coast Guard officers came to take the hijackers and smugglers away, the pickle-faced man said, "I'll be back when I get out. I have some unfinished business on this island."

"Are you threatening me?" asked Papa. "You'll see me again," answered Pickle-Face. "I'll be watching for you," promised Papa.

After that, Papa kept his revolver with him wherever he went. It was a long time before I stopped shivering whenever I saw a boat running without lights.

CHAPTER FOURTEEN

Just before Christmas Estelle came home from Bellingham. "I'm too tired to work," she said, "so Mrs. Larkin fired me."

"What makes you so tired?" asked Mamma.

"I don't know," answered Estelle. "I have pains in my knees, and arms, too. And I'm too tired to sleep nights."

"We'll get you to town for a medical examination," said Mamma. "You may have diabetes."

"I'll take her to town," said Al. He and Mary, accompanied by Estelle and Noel, left in the *Sea Pigeon* for Bellingham the following day.

When they didn't return at the time appointed, Mamma and Papa began to worry.

"Tomorrow is Christmas Eve," said Mamma. "Mary surely would want to be home."

Evening came on. We looked in vain for the approaching light that might be from the *Sea Pigeon*.

"I guess they decided to wait and come in on the morning tide," said Papa. "You'd better go to bed."

Roy, Lynn, Margaret, Thalia, and I went off to bed. Mamma thought she'd sit up and read for a while longer.

It was three o'clock in the morning when we were awakened by Estelle's long-drawn-out sobs, accompanied by the thin wailing of Noel. I hastened down the stairs. Estelle was sitting on a chair, while Papa hurried about, shaking up the coal stove to get more heat for boiling water. Mamma was stripping Noel of his wet clothing.

Seeing me, she ordered me to bring wool blankets from the upstairs closets.

I got the blankets and helped Mamma wrap Noel up. We then pulled the cold, wet clothing from Estelle, who was too cold and sick to help herself. "What happened?" I asked. Estelle continued to cry.

I helped while Mamma and Papa worked over the three chilled patients. Mamma gave them warm baths, and made Estelle and Noel swallow some brandy. Then she put them to bed, wrapped in feather ticks.

Mary was still unconscious; Mamma rubbed her body with hot oil and wrapped her warmly in a wool blanket. We wrapped hot flatirons in a flannel cloth and laid them at her feet. Mamma put two hot water bottles in the bed.

It was a whole day before either Mary or Estelle could tell us of the accident.

In the meantime, Noel had cried out, "Al's drowned in the water!"

"Where's he drowned?" asked Papa.

"In the water," answered Noel.

"Evidently he doesn't know where," said Papa, as he took his coat off the hook. "You boys come with me; we'll search the shore."

Roy and Lynn put on their jackets and followed Papa out.

After a long time, they returned.

"She's on the reef at Blanchard's Harbor," Papa said. "We made her lines fast. She's pounded up a lot on the barnacles. I'm afraid we can't beach her." He was talking about the *Sea Pigeon*.

"Any signs of Al?" asked Mamma.

"Not a thing," sorrowfully answered Papa. "I'd like to know how those youngsters got ashore from that reef; the water is neck high!"

On hearing Papa's voice, Estelle awoke from her sleep of exhaustion. "I'll tell you how it happened," she wearily said.

"We left town at nine o'clock in the morning. The water was as smooth as glass for miles out; we were laughing and talking for about an hour. Then the sky began to darken, and I said, 'There must be a storm coming. Look at the dark sky!'

"The wind came up, and the water began to act rough. It steadily got worse. The waves washed over the *Sea Pigeon,* washing the dinghy from the deck. Rain came down in sheets, and then it hailed and snowed. The engine got flooded by the big waves, and stopped. We watched the gasoline drums float away.

"We drifted until the tide washed us up on Blanchard's Reef. All our suitcases were lost; we were soaking wet, and chilled. Al decided to swim to shore and get the launch, and come back for us. He dropped over the side of the boat. In a few minutes we saw a circle of light on the water where Al had been. I don't know what happened to him. He didn't come back.

"We crawled over the slippery rocks. We slipped a lot, and were horribly scratched and bruised. We got to shore and found the cowpath. We stumbled over fallen branches in the dark. Then we lost our way in the woods. That's what took us so long to get home." Estelle lay back, weeping.

The terrible thought struck me—*I was responsible for Al's death!* I had asked God to help Mary get her love affairs straightened out.

Hurrying to my prie-dieu, I began to break up the bench. I snatched up the candles and broke them, jars and all, against the wall of the tree.

"Damn ole God—I *hate* you!"

Then, sick with weeping, I sat down to rest. I was mad clear through at God.

"Oh, God," I wailed, "you didn't have to *kill* him—you didn't have to kill *him.*"

On Christmas night, Mary opened her eyes. She sat up. "Where's Al?" she asked, staring at an empty chair beside her bed.

"He's away, Mary," answered Mamma.

"He was sitting right there a minute ago—right in that chair!" exclaimed Mary.

"No, dear; he is away," Mamma repeated, smoothing back Mary's hair. "Try to rest a while."

Mamma got up and brought a cup of hot gruel to the bedside.

She spooned some into Mary's mouth. After the gruel was all gone, Mary closed her eyes, and soon slept again.

The *Elmo* came that morning, and Papa sent a message by Captain Chase, to be telegraphed to the lighthouse headquarters, informing them of the tragedy, and asking for aid. Early the next morning, the revenue cutter *Arcata* arrived, and the Coast Guard men began to search for Al's body. The search was in vain. The men towed the *Sea Pigeon* to Bellingham and put her in dry-dock.

Papa ordered Lynn and me to stay off the beaches for a while. We knew that he was afraid of what we might find, and we were glad to stay at home.

One morning, Papa called to Mamma to come outside. They talked quietly for a moment. Then Mamma returned to the house, took her Bible from the table, her coat from a hook in the hall, and followed Papa over the hill. Papa carried a shovel and an old sail. From his actions, I sensed that Papa had found what he had been searching for. I followed at a discreet distance.

Papa and Mamma walked to Blanchard's Harbor. They stopped on the beach, put a large object into the sail, wrapped it up and together dragged it to the scrub oak at Frustration's Rendezvous. Papa dug a grave, and deposited the bundle. Mamma read from the Bible, and Papa covered the grave over. Tears rained down my face.

After Papa and Mamma had passed on their way home, I dug up a tiny fir tree.

'I'll plant it on your grave, Al," I whispered.

Approaching the grave, I was startled by running footsteps very close by. In a moment, Mary brushed past me and flung herself down on the new grave.

"Al—Al," she sobbed. I knelt beside her, placing my hand in hers.

We sobbed out our hearts at Frustration's Rendezvous.

It was several days after Al was buried that Estelle remembered to tell Mamma about her visit to the doctor.

"I almost forgot to tell you what the doctor said about me," she said. "It seems so long ago now."

"I guess we all forgot why you went to town with Al," said Mamma.

"He said I have malnutrition. I need lots of milk and eggs to build me up."

"I suspected something of the sort," said Mamma. "You evidently haven't been eating right in Bellingham. I guess you'd better remain at home for a few months, until I get you on your feet again."

When Estelle was completely recovered, she went back to work in Bellingham.

"I just can't enjoy myself being idle," she said. "Besides, Criss will be expecting me back. We hope to marry before *too* long."

Mamma wrote a letter to Billy Coutts, informing him of Al's drowning. She asked his wish concerning the disposal of the *Sea Pigeon*. We were not surprised when Billy showed up at the island in April. The details of the disaster were made known to him; he was shocked and grieved.

"The *Sea Pigeon* has been sold," Billy told Papa. "I came to see if I might be of any assistance to you—or to Mary," he added.

Papa took a long time to answer. Then he slowly spoke. "I'm much concerned over Mary. She's taking it so hard, and she is to become a mother."

"A mother!" exclaimed Billy, with shocked incredulity.

"Yes," answered Papa. "Her child will be born sometime in June."

During the evening, Billy sought out Mary as she sat on a beach log, making little ripples in the water with a stick. Mary loved to watch the phosphorescent outline of her stick, sparkling in the darkness.

Billy sat down beside her. "Beautiful, isn't it?" he asked.

Mary turned her face to him. "I thought you'd come," she said.

"I'd like to help you, Mary—you and the baby."

Mary was a long time in replying. Then she thoughtfully answered, "No, Billy. It wouldn't be right. There will be the baby, and I could never burden you with it. I'll go to work; I'm sure that I can find a position in Bellingham. I'd like to feel that I was independent."

"And the baby?" Billy spoke softly. "A baby should have a father."

Mary stood up. "Papa will keep my baby, until I am able to care for it." She turned, and began to walk away; then stopped, facing Billy again. "I don't mean to be unkind, Billy, but Al has only been gone for four months; I can't speak of any arrangement for my future without him when he's still so close to my heart. Will you excuse me, please." Mary walked swiftly to the house.

Billy sat for a long time on the log before he, too, returned to the house. He looked very unhappy as he informed Papa that he was leaving in the morning on the *Elmo*. "I may be back later in the summer," he said.

Mamma and Mary sat for long hours together, fashioning small garments for the baby. Then everything was ready, and Mamma and Mary packed the layette into suitcases. One Monday morning in late June, they left on the *Elmo* for Bellingham. We waited impatiently until the *Elmo* returned on the following Monday, bringing a letter from Mamma. Estelle opened it and read:

Dear Family:

Anita Alexandra was born on June 28. She is a beautiful little thing, with large brown eyes and wavy hair. She already has a smile, and her chin is dimpled.

Mary is doing nicely, and we shall be home on next Monday's boat.

Your loving mother.

"Anita, Anita," I murmured. "What a sweet name." "That's the name Al chose, if the baby were to be a girl," stated Estelle. "He once had a sweetheart in Spain by that name."

The great day came at last, when the baby would be brought

home. Everyone stood waiting at the boathouse when the *Elmo* came swooping through the Head-of-the-Bay passage. The steamer regained her poise, and majestically moved up to the buoy without the usual bump. We watched, as Mamma and Mary were helped down the ladder to the small boat. Then my heart sang with gladness. I saw Captain Chase reach down and hand Mamma a pink bundle.

Mary took the bundle from Mamma. Laying it onto my outstretched arms, she said, "Angie, Mamma and I have decided that Anita shall be your special charge. You will care for her, and she will be your baby. I'm going to work next week, in Bellingham."

I held her close. "My baby! My own little precious," I whispered.

I was barely thirteen when Mary gave Anita to me, but even then I had a feeling of real motherhood, and in the months that followed, Mamma said that never did a baby have better care than that which I gave Anita. I bathed her, fed her, rocked her to sleep, singing lullabies in my most doleful tones. I loved Anita, and Anita loved me.

"Lotta smoke, over there by Waldron," said Lynn, lazily rolling over on the grass. "Must be a lot of ships coming."

I looked; there *was* a great deal of smoke. We watched in silence for a while; the ships came nearer.

"It's battleships!" shouted Lynn. "Let's tell Papa." We started in search of Papa.

There is a lighthouse regulation that demands that all passing government boats must be saluted by the dipping of the flag. Also all passing government ships must be reported, as to time of passing and direction of course. These facts must be entered in the lighthouse ledger.

"Papa! Papa!" we called, through the open door of the signal. Papa didn't answer, so we ran to the house. "Mamma," we called— no answer.

"They must be down in the gardens," said Lynn. "We'll salute the ships." He untied the flag rope.

"Now," said Lynn, "when the first ship comes right in front of the flag, you let it down to quarter-mast, and then pull it up, quick."

"Oh, don't be so bossy," I said. "I've watched Papa salute as many times as you have; I know how." The four battleships approached the island. "They're flying Japanese colors," said Lynn.

"Yes, but the American ensign is flying from the stern," I answered.

As the first ship came abreast, I dipped the flag. In a moment, the American flag on the battleship dipped in answer. I was delighted. It was a thrilling experience for a young girl to be able to command a battleship to salute. Three times I saluted, as three ships passed. When the fourth ship came abreast, I saluted and received an answer.

"Oh, this is fun!" I said, and again I dipped the flag; again I was saluted by the battleship. I waited until the quartermaster had reached the bow of the ship, following the salute.

"I'll make him run back to the stern again," I said. Accordingly, I dipped the flag and, in a moment, the ship slackened speed.

At that very instant, Papa came charging up to the flagpole platform.

"What the devil are you doing?" he demanded in a very angry tone, grabbing me by the back of my dress and yanking me away from the rope. Papa quickly jerked the flag to the top of the pole and tied the rope securely. The ship proceeded on her way.

Papa grabbed me again and, turning me over his knee with no respect for my thirteen years, paddled me vigorously.

"You are not to play with the flag," he said. "You know how to salute properly. That quartermaster shouldn't have been forced to salute more than once. You've sure put me in a bad light with that Jap ship."

CHAPTER FIFTEEN

I knew that I shouldn't be eavesdropping. I had been lectured and punished a great many times for indulging in the disgraceful habit, but I was a very stubborn child, and grownups had so many interesting things to say. So I lay behind the sofa and listened to Papa and his friends from the Coast Guard cutter *Guard*, as they played cards and talked.

"I hear that one of the hijackers you turned in a while back is being turned loose in a few days, Ed." It was Captain Black talking. "And we've got our orders to be on the lookout for him. I hear tell he promised you he'd be back here to settle an old score."

"Pickle-Face?" asked Papa. His voice sounded strange to me, as if he were afraid.

"Yes, he's the one."

"He did threaten to come back and finish up some business on Patos, but I didn't take him seriously. You really think he'll be back?"

"That's what the general opinion seems to be. We had orders yesterday to be alert."

"Well, I'll be damned," swore Papa. "I didn't think he'd be out gunning for me. He thinks I killed his brother, though, and he'll try to even the score. I'll be watching."

I couldn't very well crawl out from behind the couch while the men were still there, so I put my hands under my head and fell asleep.

When I awoke, it was dark and still in the house. The men had gone and the family was asleep. I felt sore and stiff from lying on the floor. Just as I began to crawl out from my hiding place, I heard the floor creak as if someone were tiptoeing through the room. I felt a chill go up my spine.

"Pickle-Face," I thought.

I listened while the soft pad, pad, pad of the feet went past the couch and on into the parlor. Then I crept out and tiptoed into the kitchen. I was just going to open the door to the hall that led upstairs when the door opened from the other side. The owner of the tiptoeing feet had come into the hall from the parlor.

I screamed as loud as I could—"Papa! Papa! Pickle-Face has got me!" And then I fainted dead away.

When I came to, Mamma was holding me in her arms. "Whatever made you scream? And what are you doing up at two thirty in the morning? I was just walking around in the dark to quiet my nerves, when I am suddenly frightened out of my wits by your screams. I do find you in the most surprising places, Angel. Whatever ails you, that you don't behave like a proper child?"

"Oh, Mamma, I thought that Pickle-Face, the hijacker, was here after Papa, and I'm so scared." I began to cry hard. Mamma led me up to bed.

One afternoon shortly after my nightmare about Pickle-Face, I was resting under a madroña tree at Frustration's Rendezvous. The day was warm and I fell asleep and had another dream about pirates. This is the dream I dreamed.

The boat came straight in until her bow touched the gravel of the beach. I watched the five men climb over her sides and wade to the shore. They were dressed in oilskins, and three of them carried shovels. Straight up the bank they marched, and toward my resting place. I tried to arise from my bed of leaves; my body seemed to be rooted to the spot; I couldn't move.

The leader of the men stood before me. "We'll bury them there," he said. "Dig one large grave."

Three of the men began to shovel the leaves away, and then to dig. When they were through with their work, a long, deep hole lay open near my feet.

"Come on," said the leader. "We'll get the bodies." Straight to the boat they walked. In horror, I watched as six white corpses were tossed to the beach! With a man at the head and one at the feet, two of the corpses were carried to the place where I lay. I watched while they threw the bodies into the grave. Piled like cordwood, one on top of the other, the dead men's open eyes looked into mine, and I felt that I, too, was a cold, white corpse. In vain, I tried to escape; I struggled against the something that bound me to the spot. Cold fear took possession of me and I sank back on the leaves, tired and exhausted.

"Cover them up," the leader commanded. The men turned and went back to the boat.

"What'll we do with *him*?" I heard a voice ask.

"Kill him and bury him, too," suggested another.

"No," said the leader, "we don't kill youngsters. Lay him on the beach; give him some water. He's too sick to live long, and he'll die anyway."

The men carried a young boy from the boat, and stretched him out on the beach. Someone set a demijohn beside him. The five men climbed into the boat, shoved off and disappeared around the point.

After a long time, the boy moaned; his hand reached out for the water. He tipped the demijohn and tried to drink but he was too weak to bring the water to his mouth.

"I'll help you," I said. I tried to run to him; my feet wouldn't budge.

"Never mind," he said, "I'll be better in a moment." Some time later, the boy pushed himself to his knees, reached for the demijohn, and spilled a little water into his mouth. He crawled toward me, crossing the newly made grave, and made his way to the tree where I was lying.

"I'll put it here," he said, "in this hole in the tree, above you. When I am gone, you must promise to get it and send it back home."

"I promise," I said, "but what is it?"

"It's my ancestral jade," he answered. "I stole it from my grandfather's tomb. It is thousands of years old, and carries a curse for all who wrongfully possess it."

The boy sank down under the tree; he seemed to disappear into the earth.

"Where are you? Where are you?" I cried.

"Woof! Woof!" barked Curly. He began to dig in the leaves under the tree. I sat up with a jerk, as the leaves and dirt struck my face.

"Curly, stop that!" I commanded. Curly backed away from the spot, growling and whining at something. There wasn't a thing in sight, except the old tree, yet Curly was seeing something that was not visible to me. Then—I stared at the ground where I had been resting. There, uncovered by Curly's digging, lay a human skull. I shivered.

"I had a terrible dream, Curly," I said. "A boy put something in a hole in a tree—a hole in that very tree!"

After dinner, I told the family about the dream.

"You shouldn't go to sleep in the scrub oak grove," admonished Papa. "Too many smugglers' graves down there, and Chinese, too. Some of those dead Chinese might jump out at you," he winked at Mamma.

"Don't scare her, Ed," said Mamma.

"But I am scared, Mamma," I said. "There is a hole in the tree, right over the place where I saw the skull."

Papa laughed, "Why don't you crawl in and see what's in the hole?" He thought the whole tale very funny.

Later in the evening, Lynn asked me to tell about the dream again. When I had finished, he said, "Let's go down and look in the hole tomorrow."

"I'm afraid," I said.

"I'm not," answered Lynn, "and I mean to have a look."

Early the next morning, we called Curly and set out for the scrub oak. We walked straight to the large madroña tree, under which I had slept. As we approached the spot, Curly began to sniff and whine, backing away from the place.

Standing on tiptoe, Lynn reached into the hollowed trunk of the tree, and brought out a small, wooden box! There was a rusted lock fastening the lid of the box, and Lynn was unable to force it open. It was a beautifully carved box, made of sandalwood.

"Oh, how pretty!" I said, reaching for the carved box.

"God damn," said Lynn, "looks awfully old. We'll take it to Papa."

"Papa," I said, as we entered the barn where Papa was working, "Lynn found this box in the tree trunk, right over the place where I saw the sick boy."

"What lies are you telling now?" roared Papa. He took the box from my hand and pried open the rusted lock.

Inside the box was a square of thin silk, upon which were written some Chinese words. Papa laid the silk aside and lifted out a package wrapped in rough, waxed paper, sealed with heavy wax. Breaking the seal, he tore off the wrapping. Inside was still another wrapping of oiled silk. Papa unfolded the silk. His face turned white as he lifted out a jade scarab.

"My God!" Papa swore. "A Chinese burying charm. A curse to all who wrongfully come by it. Lynn, where did you find this?"

"Right in the hole that Angie dreamed about," said Lynn. "The sick boy must have put it there."

Papa exploded. "God-damn-it, Angie. At a time like this, why can't you tell the truth? You and your dreams," he scornfully added.

Papa knew a great deal about Chinese charms. He had been told about the jade scarabs by the Chinese at the customs house in Port Townsend. He was in great agitation over the sandalwood box and its contents.

In their bedroom that night, I heard Papa ask Mamma, "Now, how in the world did that child know that the box was in that madroña tree, or what its contents were?"

"She's psychic. I'm sure that the Chinese boy visited her in her dream," answered Mamma.

In a few days, Papa went to Port Townsend to the customs office. He showed them the note and the scarab. A Chinese interpreter was called in.

"We must return it to China," he said, "lest a curse fall upon us."

Papa gladly handed over the sandalwood box, with its contents.

Another winter passed and in the spring Bully went on a rampage.

"Oh, it was awful," wept Margaret. "I was way up there, and Papa was on the ground, and Bully jumped and pawed—"

"Start from the beginning and quit crying," I snapped. Papa was lying in his bed, battered and bruised, with four broken ribs. The doctor had been with him all day long, and still Papa was in no condition to be moved to a hospital.

"I was just walking home by the path," said Margaret, "when Bully came out of the woods. I ran to the smokehouse. The ladder was there and I climbed it fast. Bully came into the smokehouse. He stood still a minute and sniffed. His nose was pointed up to the ceiling. Then he saw me and swished his tail and snorted, and then began to bump the ladder with his horns.

"'Papa!' I yelled. 'Curly,' I shouted. Curly came, and Bully tried to hook him. Bully was bellowing and Curly was barking real loud. I screamed and screamed, 'Papa! Papa!'

"Papa came into the doorway. Bully ran at Papa and knocked him down. Papa fell on his face and lay still. Bully jumped on Papa and hooked him. Then God came in the smokehouse door. He had a pitchfork in his hand. He stuck it in Bully's flanks real hard.

"Bully ran out the door, and Curly bit him. God felt Papa all over, and then climbed up and brought me down. Then he closed the smokehouse door and went into the woods. I ran home to get Mamma, and the wheelbarrow to pick Papa up in. I met Billy Coutts on the way. Oh, it was awful," and Margaret began to cry again.

"I know the rest," I said.

Papa was black and blue all over and terribly swollen. "I'll stay here tonight," said the doctor, "as moving him before the bleeding stops would be pretty dangerous. Besides, he's suffering from shock."

"It's a good thing Billy happened along to help us," said Mamma. "He was looking for Papa in the barn when he heard the commotion."

"Mamma, it was Angel's God," Margaret said. "An old man God just like Angel always talks about."

"Whatever are you saying?" asked Mamma. "I think Angel has been teaching you her peculiar ways."

"No, Mamma, I really saw old God, myself. He was wearing Papa's old coat; the one you tried to find a long time ago. He was wearing it, and he had long, white hair."

"Oh, please hush, Margaret. I'm too worried about Papa to contend with your silly notions—you were so upset you couldn't be sure."

"But who did drive the bull away?" asked Billy. "Why—I supposed you did—didn't you?" asked Mamma.

"No, I did not," answered Billy.

I took Margaret outside. "Did you really see God?" I asked her.

"I saw a funny old man," she answered. "He picked Bully with a pitchfork."

"Please don't tell Mamma anything more about him," I said. "She'll think you're queer like me."

"I won't—ever!" promised Margaret.

It was several days before Papa was moved to a hospital, and several weeks before he returned home. In the meantime, the new assistant keeper who was to take Al's place had arrived, and he and Mamma ran the lighthouse.

When Papa came home from the hospital, he went directly to his room and changed into his overalls.

"You must rest," warned Mamma. "You've had a hard pull, and you're still not out of danger."

"I'll not rest," declared Papa, taking his service revolver from under his pillow, "until I shoot that goddamn bull!"

The new assistant keeper, Mr. Cook, carried Papa's rifle, and together they went in search of Bully.

CHAPTER SIXTEEN

Again the warm summer days settled over the island. Patos slumbered in the warm caress of the sun. There were fewer of the family home for the holidays than in previous years. Roy had taken a job in town; Mary and Estelle also were living in a faraway city. Our family had dwindled to Lynn, Margaret, Thalia, Noel, and myself—and, of course, baby Anita.

Mary and Billy came home for a visit. Mary brought Anita a large cuddly bear.

"What a good little mother you've become, Angie," praised Mary. "My baby looks wonderful!"

One evening, a few days later, I walked on the bank, near the old twisted tree. As I approached the tree, I heard voices. I didn't especially care about listening, but I sat down nearby, to watch the lights of a passing ship. The waves made little lapping noises on the shore. The heaven was bright with stars. It was an evening of enchantment. I heard Billy's soft voice speaking.

> The twinkling stars, the breezes from the sea
> And you beside me, must ever be
> As enduring as these. My sweet,
> I love you with all my heart and soul.

"Oh, Billy, that's beautiful," exclaimed Mary.

"I wrote it especially for you, Mary. I've waited a year to tell you—Mary, I want you for my wife."

"So that's it," I said, turning away. "All these years he has said that I was the one he loved." I ran straight to my room and, throwing myself on my bed, began to sob.

Mamma came to the bedside. "Angie," she asked, "whatever is the matter?" I told her about Billy and Mary.

"Angie," Mamma spoke softly, stroking my hot forehead, "Billy has been in love with Mary for several years. He is twenty years older than you; his love for you was the love for a little sister. You're too young for love, Angie; someday you'll see the difference."

Mamma kissed me and went out. I felt a great sense of peace and contentment settle over me after she left, and I fell asleep without bothering to undress.

On Monday, Mary and Billy left on the *Elmo* for Bellingham.

A few days after Mary's visit, we were surprised to see a small motorboat draw up to the rocks, in front of the house. Motorboats usually came into the bay.

The skipper of the boat stood up and waved his hand at us, calling, "Telegram."

Lynn rushed down to hear what he was saying, and returned a moment later with a yellow envelope in his hand.

Mamma shook a little as she opened the envelope. "Oh, my goodness!" she said. "It's Roy!" She dropped the telegram and rushed indoors.

Papa picked it up. "Read it," he ordered.

I read:

ROY IN HOSPITAL STOP TUBERCULOSIS KNEE STOP
AMPUTATION NECESSARY COME AT ONCE.
                                        MARY.

Mamma came out of the house. "Ed, have the messenger wait," she said. "I'm going in with him to East Sound; I'll catch the *Chippewa* there, and go on to Bellingham."

CHAPTER SIXTEEN ⁀

Papa ran down to the shore to make the necessary arrangements. The messenger waited while Papa helped Mamma pack. As she packed, she talked rapidly.

"I'll get in touch with headquarters and have a man sent out to relieve you, Ed; you must come to town on the *Elmo* Monday. Angie and Margaret are capable of running the house for a few days. Ask Mr. Cook to do your chores, and Mrs. Cook to board the relief man. I don't want him here with the children. Lynn can help with the stock, and take care of the fires." Mamma was off in a whirling rush. She didn't stop to kiss any of us good-bye.

It was two days before Papa's relief came. Papa gave him complete instructions concerning the lighthouse; he was to report to Mr. Cook for orders. On Monday, Papa left for Bellingham.

There was a letter for me in the mail; it was from Mamma. She wrote a lengthy, detailed order as to how I was to run the house in her absence this time.

On the following Monday, Papa and Mamma returned.

"Roy's leg was amputated," Mamma said. "They cut it off above the knee."

Lynn, Margaret, and I were saddened to learn of Roy's misfortune. We tried to imagine the gay, reckless, always laughing Roy—with only one leg.

Roy came home in late August. We were all lined up at the boathouse; our faces were grave and sorrowful.

"That's the way we should look," I told Margaret, Thalia, and Noel. "He wouldn't want us to look happy, when he has only one leg."

We saw Roy as he handed down his crutches to Papa and slid down the ladder to the small boat.

Soon they were ashore; we waited breathlessly. It was going to be a shock to see Roy without his cheery smile. Hopping out of the boat, Roy took his crutches from Papa's hand and began to hobble toward us.

When he was almost to the spot where we quietly waited, he

stopped, waved his hand and shouted, his face breaking out into a cheerful grin. "H'lo, kids; gee, wait till you see all the tricks I can do on these wonderful crutches!"

Our solemn looks vanished.

"Why," I said, "Roy hasn't changed a bit; he's as funny as ever."

We clambered about him then, begging to be allowed to try out his crutches. Those crutches became a source of delight to all of us.

"Did it hurt bad—when they cut it off?" I asked Roy, concerning his leg.

"No, not much, only it did afterward, quite a bit." His face brightened. "But you should see all the gifts I got. My bed was loaded with all sorts of things, and all our friends came to see me. I had a lot of fun in the hospital."

Roy soon adjusted himself to existing conditions, and was again his cheerful self. He began to learn the shoemaker's trade from Papa.

One Monday, Estelle and Criss came home on the *Elmo*.

"We're going to be married, Mamma," Estelle announced. "Clara wants us to have the wedding at her home; she's a little lonesome. So I consented. Have you any objections?" she asked.

"No," answered Mamma, "but we can't take all the children to Clara's."

"It's to be a very simple wedding," said Estelle. "Why can't just you and Papa come?" So, we were left at home again, while Mamma and Papa went to Estelle's wedding.

It was a week later that Mary and Billy came home.

"We've come to take Anita," she said. "We're going to Alaska to live."

"*Anita,*" I shouted. "You gave Anita to me! Don't you remember? Anita is *my* baby; you can't take her back now; you can't be an Indian giver! Mamma," I appealed, "she can't take Anita away; tell her she can't!"

"Angie," Mamma spoke softly. "Anita is Mary's baby—her first-born. She didn't mean that you could *have* Anita; she merely left her in your care. No, Angie, Anita is not your child."

I was shocked. Unbelieving that anyone could do such a terrible thing, I screamed, "No!" and ran out of the house.

I didn't stop running until I had reached Al's grave, in the scrub oak. Throwing myself over the grave, I sobbed, "Oh, Al—Al—they're taking Anita away from me—my own little baby—they're taking her away." I sobbed loudly, my whole body shaking with grief.

Suddenly, I heard a soft voice say, "Everything's all right, Angie—all right—all right."

I stood up; there was no one in sight. All at once, I felt calm; at peace. "Yes, I heard you, Al," I whispered. "I'll give Anita up to her mother."

For the next few days I played with Anita a lot. I brushed her curls, turning them over in my fingers lovingly. I kissed her, petted her. I thought I'd have to give her enough to last her a long time.

"I'll bring her back, every summer," promised Mary, "and I'll send pictures of her each month."

This didn't entirely console me; I still felt that parting with the baby was a terrible ordeal.

I tied Anita's pink ruffled bonnet, put on the pink coat, and kissed her.

"Goin' bye-bye—goin' bye-bye—" she chanted. My heart was heavy.

Mary picked her up and began to walk to the boathouse. I didn't go down to the boathouse with them. I thought I couldn't bear to see Anita go. I walked to the fog signal; climbed the tower stairs.

Roy was shining the lens. "H'lo, kid," he cheerfully greeted me.

"H'lo," I answered.

"Why all the gloom?" he asked.

"Oh, nothing," I answered, "I'm just wondering what life will bring to me during the next few years; I wonder—"

"Stop wondering," said Roy. "We all get tough breaks, but we don't whine. The worth-while man is the one who can sing himself out of his gloom. Come on—let's sing now."

Roy began, "Some think the world was made for fun and frolic, and so do I—and so do I—"

I joined in on the chorus, "Hearken, hearken, music—tra la la la la—tra la la la—" We were both laughing and singing together.

Papa and Mamma were standing beside Mamma's dresser. They were looking at an old newspaper that was spread out. "He must be pretty old now," Papa said. "I don't suppose he'd be recognized even if I did find him."

"Why do you persist in your old dream, Ed?" asked Mamma. "We have done quite well on the island. We have almost accomplished our purpose. Our family is nearly all off our hands. Why do you want to catch Spanish John?"

"Because I have always wanted the glory of bringing him in," Papa answered. "I have never given up hope of getting off this island. You've had your way, but at what a cost. We've lost five of our family, and had one crippled. I feel that it never would have happened in town."

"Worse might have happened in town," Mamma answered. "Nutrition is very important in the lives of children. Perhaps they might have all died of malnutrition. I still feel that we did the right thing."

I entered the room. "I'm glad we've lived on Patos," I said. "It's so lovely here—I never want to leave as long as God is—" I stood directly in front of the picture of Spanish John. I stood staring at the eyes. "The eyes—the eyes—" I stammered.

"Sh-h—" Mamma put her fingers to her lips and looked sternly at me. "Please leave, Angel," she said.

"But, Mamma, I've seen those eyes—" suddenly I remembered something. I ran from the room; down the stairs I fled, and out the front door.

As fast as I could I ran to my prie-dieu tree. Before I entered the cave I called, "God! God! I have to talk to you. God—hurry up!" Then I stooped down and entered the cave.

CHAPTER SIXTEEN ∾

Someone grabbed me and held my mouth shut. I couldn't see him very well, because of the dim light in the cave. I kicked and squirmed and finally got my head loose.

"God! God!" I yelled. I wriggled out of the cave, but not before the person inside grabbed my foot.

Lucky for me that I had been an outdoor girl for so many years. I was very strong. I held tight to a root of the old tree. In a moment Pickle-Face crawled out of the cave.

"Now, you tell me who this God is, and where he is hiding," he commanded.

"No, no—I won't," I sobbed.

He slapped me so hard that my ears were ringing. I felt sick, but I determined to die before I told on God.

"Where is he?" he asked. "I've been watching you out here for three days. You always bring food in this tree, and you are always talking to someone. I've hunted, but I can't find him—where is he?"

"I just *pretend*," I said. "There isn't really anyone here; I just pretend."

"You're a liar, kid," he said. "I have ears—I heard a man's voice—"

"Here's the man!" and God stood before us.

"John! You damned murderer!" shouted Pickle-Face. He drew a knife from his belt and threw it at God. It struck God in his chest. He shuddered and sat slowly down.

"Don't be hasty, Lyle," he spoke softly. "You hardly know the facts of the case. I—"

"You're a murderer. You killed my brother, and I'm going to finish you now."

"Not so fast, my friend!" I whirled around and there stood Papa and Mamma. Papa pointed a pistol at Pickle-Face. Mamma held a rope in her hands.

"Stand where you are," Papa said. "Tie him up, Estelle." Mamma moved over to where Pickle-Face stood, and securely tied his hands and feet. Then she ran to God.

"John, John," she sobbed. "I didn't dream a thing like this would happen, or I wouldn't have urged you to remain on the island. Oh, I'm so sorry—"

"It's all right—everything's all right," answered God. "It had to happen sometime. I am a very old man. Rest assured that my last few years have been most gratifying ones. Playing God to this little girl has given me peace and joy. I can go to my Maker with a clear conscience.

"I have been a smuggler, yes; but I have never been a murderer, before.

"I killed Carl Sancho, the brother of Lyle here, because he stole my boat and cargo. He tied me to a plank and left me to die at sea. Fortunately I drifted in at Blanchard's Harbor. Blanchard nursed me through the illness that followed. I lived in his cabin until you folks came to Patos. Then I hid out in the log house in the swamp. I have a cave under this tree. You'll find a rope ladder hanging over the bank. It's behind that cedar tree." He pointed to a nearby cedar.

"There's a box of jewelry in the log house. It belonged to my father, who was a pirate in these waters long ago. He named this island Patos. At first he called it Perdita, because it is so lost from the other San Juans. Grandfather was the original San Juan Islander.

"I'd leave the jewels to Angel, but they'd only bring her unhappiness. They've brought unhappiness to all who have owned them.

"The fishing tackle and other gear in this cave I give to Lynn. He has befriended me in many ways."

"Lynn knew?" asked Mamma.

"Yes," said God. "He knew from the very first. He's a good boy. He can keep a secret. He knew that it was I who put the Chinese scarab in the tree so Angel would find it. Just to make her dream come true."

I recovered from my astonishment. "John—Spanish John— *you?* You're not God?" Tears welled in my eyes. "Not—God—" I stammered.

Papa had been silent throughout this little tableau. Now he began to speak.

"Mamma just told me, Angel. She knew you were heading here when you saw John's picture. We followed you here. Mamma has been watching nights for Pickle-Face for several months. She saw him skulking around yesterday. She knew he would be at your prie-dieu."

"How did you know, Mamma?" I asked.

"I listened to the Coast Guardsmen that night I frightened you almost to death, when you were skulking around in the dark. I've watched every night since," she said. "I found out about John after the bull got Papa in the smokehouse. I came here and began to talk to him."

Spanish John opened his eyes. "If you'll remove the knife from my wound, I'll be off," he said.

"No! No!" I screamed. "Don't leave me—I'm so used to you—"

"I have to go, Angel. You won't—need me—now. You—can—pray to—the real—God, and—your parents understand you—at last." He closed his eyes again—his words came slower, softly.

"Cremate me—like you did the sea gull, Angel. Make—them—do it—that way. Then—you—toss my ashes—over the waves. I want—to be free—forever free—" Spanish John and God left Patos Island.

Papa made the hijacker walk to the bay, where he was turned over to the Coast Guard.

They removed the body of Spanish John to Bellingham. After it had been cremated, Papa brought the ashes back. I tossed them over the waves on a windy day.

"Return to the sea—the sea you loved, God of my childhood prayers. Float free with the wind and the whispering waves, washed clean from worldly cares."

Then I whispered, "Forever free, Spanish John—never hunted again—free—forever free." I wept.

"Come up to the house, Angel." Mamma took my arm and led me away.

"You are to go with Papa and me to Blanchard's cabin. Spanish John told me that under the floor is hidden a large cache of opium. I've known all about it for a long time, but I didn't want Papa to find John, and so end our days at Patos. I learned to love your 'God' as much as you did."

"Will Papa get the reward money?" I asked. "No," answered Mamma. "No one will receive that. You see, the hijacker really led the Coast Guard officers to Spanish John. They have known he was here for several months. They didn't want to bring him in because of your faith in him."

"Poor Papa," I murmured. "He never gets his way."

"Papa has the wrong attitude," snapped Mamma.

We reached the house, where Papa was waiting with the tools necessary for breaking open Blanchard's cabin.

"I haven't been near the old cabin for years," Papa said. "I wonder if I can find it since the underbrush has grown so high about it."

"I forgot all about the old cabin, too," I answered. "You told us children to keep away from it years ago, and we did."

"That's the only thing you ever did that I told you to," said Papa.

Mamma didn't make any comments at all. She walked rapidly on in the lead. In a short time she led us straight to the cabin.

"Why, there's a path, quite a worn path going in here," Papa was astonished.

"Yes," explained Mamma. "John and I made it. He always wintered here. Al used to bring him supplies." "Al did?" asked Papa.

"Yes. Al knew about John, but at that time I didn't. John told me the whole story a short time ago. He and Al were friends the last two years of Al's life."

Papa didn't need the tools for opening up the cabin; it was already unlocked. We went in.

"Under the old rocker," Mamma directed. "That's where John said it was hidden."

CHAPTER SIXTEEN ~

Papa moved the rocker aside and lifted the rug from the floor.

Picking up the loose floor boards, he knelt, reached down into a large hole and took out several tobacco cans. Inside the cans were dozens of small boxes marked "quinine." They contained little capsules filled with white powder.

"It's opium, no doubt," said Papa, "but in this refined powder form, we call it morphine."

We carried the morphine to the lighthouse, where the officers of the Guard took charge of it. After a long hunt we found the log cabin in the swamp.

"All these years I've lived here, I never guessed this cabin was here," Papa said.

The box of jewels was uncovered: emeralds, jade, rubies.

"They must be worth a great deal of money," said Mamma.

"I wonder how many poor beggars had to die for them," mused Papa. "Jewels are a curse to the world. Women sell their souls— men murder for them."

"What shall we do with them?" asked Mamma. "For my part, I don't want anything to do with them."

"I'll take them to Seattle and sell them," said Papa. "It's been so many years ago since they were stolen that no one *could* claim them now. I'll sell them cheap."

In a few weeks, Papa received a check for $1,000 for the recovery of the morphine. He folded the check and put it carefully away.

"Now you can leave Patos, Papa," I said. "You have a thousand dollars now. You can start a shoestore."

"Angel," he answered, "sometimes the things a man sets his heart on in his youth don't mean the same to him when he's older. I don't want to leave Patos now. It has memories—and voices."

"Papa!" I exclaimed in surprise. "Do you feel like I do about Patos? Do you hear the trees, the sea, the winds, and the grasses talking?"

"Yes, I do," he answered. "Only a few people ever hold so close a communion with nature. It's a kinship with—God, I think."

It was lonely on the island after Anita went away. Lynn returned to Bellingham to school; Margaret was interested in learning to sew; Thalia was ten years old now, and Mamma was teaching her to cook. Noel was entirely devoted to Roy, and followed him everywhere. I was almost alone.

I studied my French and algebra; Mamma wanted me to go to a girls' school next year, and I wished to make a good showing there. I worked diligently over my books.

In midwinter, Mamma received a letter from Clara. She was expecting a baby, and would Mamma please come?

"Of course, I'll go," said Mamma. She sat down and wrote Clara a long letter.

Mamma was gone for three weeks. I helped the younger children with their lessons, and kept the house clean. Papa helped Margaret with the cooking.

When Mamma returned, she was very tired. "Ed," she said, "I think we should get a transfer to a place near the city; Angie should go to school, and Margaret and Thalia, too. We have money saved; you have the thousand from the Spanish John loot, also five hundred dollars from the sale of the jewels. And we've saved about three thousand dollars from our salary. You can set yourself up in the shoe business like you've always wanted to. I think Patos has served its purpose for us."

Papa looked shocked. "Hell!" he swore. "For ten years I've fought to leave Patos. I used every argument possible to convince you that we should go. Now, by hell, I won't go. I *love* the island. I won't go!"

"I've already made all the arrangements," Mamma said. "We'll go to Semiahmoo Harbor Lighthouse at first. Then you can look around for something to suit yourself. You can buy your shoestore and let Roy run it for a while. He will need such a job."

"Damn-it-to-hell—I won't go to Semiahmoo Lighthouse. That little birdhouse perched up on stilts at Blaine. It's a mile out in the sea from town. I won't go. I won't," Papa wailed.

But I knew he *would* go. Mamma always got her way. I was sick at heart.

Mamma already had Papa's appointment for the lighthouse at Semiahmoo Harbor, near Blaine, Washington. It was a lighthouse built on piles, about a mile from shore.

"We'll buy a house in town for Lynn and Noel and the girls and myself," Mamma told Papa. "Roy and you will live at the lighthouse. After you get established in the shoe business, Roy can run the lighthouse in your place."

Papa thought this a capital idea. They accepted the offer of Semiahmoo, and began preparations for moving.

"The cows have to be disposed of," Papa said. "We'll try to sell them."

Mr. Cook, the new keeper, wanted to keep two of the cows, so Papa sold him two of the younger ones. All of the others, and also Bill, the horse, were sold to a farmer on Orcas Island. The farmer also bought most of our chickens, pigs, geese, and ducks.

When the scow in which the cows were to be transferred to Orcas arrived, I was very sad. Some of them, including René's Snowball, had become close friends of mine. I wept to see them go.

In the busy days that followed, I was torn between conflicting desires. I didn't want to leave my beloved island. On the other hand, I wanted to know what life in the city was like; to go to real churches, with organ music; have boys and girls of my own age for companions; high school, parties, and many other promising experiences.

I took long walks, with Curly as my only companion. I touched beloved rocks, spoke to my pets along the trail.

"I don't want to leave you," I whispered. "I'll never forget you."

I took half a sack of wheat and sowed it in the woods, near Millie the mouse's tree home. "Just in case you need food some cold winter," I told her. I wondered if the new keeper would find Millie and kill her.

I visited Al's grave. "I'll never forget you," I promised.

The day of our departure arrived. Our household goods were loaded on the *Heather,* and we were ready to leave our island. I tied a rope to Curly's collar and, leading him, followed the others to the shore, where the lifeboats waited. In a few minutes, we were waving good-bye to Patos.

I stood on the stern of the *Heather,* until the island was a tiny speck in the distance. All the joys and sorrows of the past ten years crowded into my thoughts. I remembered when Patos waved a welcome to me, when I was five; the face in the woods; God; the cows, Florabelle and Charm; the voice of the island that spoke to me so often; the Chinese jewel; my lonely walks—all the things that had made up my life.

The tears were coming fast now. "I'll never forget you," I said aloud.

"Why the tears?" asked Papa, standing beside me.

I started—then leaned on the rail again. "Oh, Papa, it's just that I remember Patos Island," I said.

Papa took my hand. "Good-bye, Paradise," he whispered.

And Mamma, who had insisted on bringing us to Patos, didn't even look back.

Helene Glidden

Who was Helene Glidden? Were the events described in this book historically accurate or were they just a childhood fantasy? Did her family really live on Patos Island? Was her father a lighthouse keeper and did he, in fact, save sailors from a shipwreck on the rocks? Whatever happened to "Angie" and her family?

It is impossible to read *The Light on the Island* and not have questions. This curiosity can lead one on a journey as fascinating as the book itself. If one researches maritime books, old newspaper clippings and visits the Coast Guard and Maritime Museums, it is possible to gain a glimpse of what truly happened in the early part of the last century on Patos Island.

James A. Gibbs has written many wonderful maritime books. His extensive research has preserved an important part of our nation's lighthouse history. His books *Sentinels of the Pacific* (Binfords & Mort, 1955), *West Coast Lighthouses* (Superior Publishing Company, 1974) and *Lighthouses of the Pacific* (Schiffer Publishing, 1986) all make helpful references to Mrs. Glidden's *The Light on the Island*.

Mr. Gibbs provides the true identity of "Edward and Estelle LaBrege" as Edward and Estelle Durgan. An August 26, 1951 *Seattle Times* book review of *The Light on the Island* clarifies Mrs. Glidden's choice of the surname "LaBrege" for her story. The article explains that her father changed his last name from "LaBrege" to "Durgan" when he emigrated to the United States from France.

The lighthouse at Turn Point on Stuart Island. *Photo courtesy of Puget Sound Maritime Historical Society*

In the late 1800's, Ed Durgan served at the Coquille River and Heceta Head Lighthouses in Oregon before moving his family north to Washington.

On the evening of February 16, 1897 at the Turn Point Lighthouse on Stuart Island in the San Juans, Mr. Durgan and his Assistant Keeper, Peter M. Christiansen, heard the repeated blasts of a ship's whistle. They found a tugboat run aground on the rocks and immediately grabbed their pikepoles and waded into the chilly water. Mysteriously there was no one on the *Enterprise's* deck, but the keeper's shouts eventually awoke the captain from his slumber.

The recently restored Turn Point Lighthouse keeper's residence on Stuart Island where the Durgan Family lived in 1897. *Photo by Michael D. McCloskey*

The crew of recently hired drifters from Port Townsend were heavily intoxicated and of no help. After a great struggle the two keepers and Ed Simms, the ship's captain, secured the boat in a cove nearby. To add to the chaos, one of the crew members went berserk with a butcher knife and had to be chained in the light station's hen house.

Both men were presented a Letter of Commendation, dated March 1, 1897 by the United States Navy for their *"heroic conduct in rendering assistance to the officers and crew of the ... Enterprise of Port Townsend, Wash., which was wrecked near Stuart Island on the evening of 16 February, '97, whereby all lives on board the vessel were saved. Such services to humanity merit the highest commendation, and the Board is glad to number among its employees men of such sterling courage and fidelity to duty, who are willing to jeopardize their own lives in order to save the lives of others."*

In 1900, Helene (Durgan) Glidden was born at the New Dungeness Lighthouse on the Strait of Juan de Fuca where her father was stationed. She was the seventh of thirteen children. The family's move to Patos Island in 1905 was out of necessity and resisted by her father. He dreaded the remote location and knew he would be rowing 25 miles to Bellingham for supplies.

Patos Island, 207 heavily wooded acres, was discovered in 1792 by the Spanish explorers Dionisio Galiano and Cayetano Valdez in the schooners *Sutil* and *Mexicana*. They were assisting Lieutenant Francisco Eliza in charting the San Juan Islands. The explorers named the small island, the northernmost of the San Juan Archipelago, *Isla de Patos* or "Island of Ducks."

The Patos Island Lighthouse, established on Alden Point in 1893, was managed by the U.S. Lighthouse Service until the department merged with the Coast Guard in 1939. The Greek Revival/Victorian style wood signal building, with a third class Daboll horn, was constructed in 1898. A 35-foot light tower was added in 1908. The original Fourth Order Fresnel Lens is currently on display at the Admiralty Head Lighthouse at Fort Casey State Park on Whidbey Island.

Chapters Six and Nine of *The Light on the Island* refer to a "Colonel Theodore Roosevelt" writing and visiting the LaBrege family on Patos. In one letter he told Ed LaBrege that the U.S. fleet of sixteen battleships would pass the Patos Island Lighthouse on June 20. Historical records quote President Roosevelt as believing, "the Navy . . . is the right arm of the United States and is emphatically the peacemaker." He nearly doubled its size and sent the fleet around the world from 1907-1909 to showcase its military strength. Historical records also confirm a visit by the U.S. fleet to the State of Washington in the first year of the journey.

Did President Roosevelt actually visit Patos Island? According to the Roche Harbor Resort archives, President Roosevelt visited the Hotel de Haro on July 13, 1906 and August 12, 1907. It is entirely possible that he would stop to see an old friend on a neighboring island.

The death of one of the Durgan's children was confirmed in a 1910 *Bellingham Herald* obituary. It lists Cecil Durgan passing away on January 10, 1910. This would be the "René" in Helene's story, who died of appendicitis.

Angie's encounters with an island historian named Mr. Blanchard, who lived on the other end of Patos, are confirmed by noted historian and author Lucille S. McDonald. Her 1990 book, *Making History: The People Who Shaped the San Juan Islands*, mentions an elderly recluse named E.B. Blanchard whose cabin stood at the east end of Patos Island. She also confirms the stories of smugglers hiding in Active Cove, where many of Angie's episodes take place.

Although most of the San Juan Islands have been logged over the last century, Patos has remained virtually untouched. A hike around the island today will reveal hundreds of fallen, rotting trees beneath a thick canopy of tall evergreens. There are few tree stumps, a tell-tale sign of past logging. The thick salal leads one to believe that Spanish John, or "God," could easily have hidden from Angie's family.

"Papa" sadly whispered "Good-bye, Paradise" as he moved his family to Bellingham in 1913. A 1919 *Bellingham Herald* article reported the sudden death of Edward Durgan on March 20 at the age of 60. Born on September 15, 1858, Mr. Durgan died of a heart attack pulling his launch up the boat ramp at the Semiahmoo Lighthouse in Blaine, Washington, where he was a keeper.

His wife Estelle tried to signal for help, over a mile and a half away, but to no avail. In spite of her husband's condition, she honored her oath as an assistant keeper by "remaining at her post until relieved." Mr. Durgan's obituary listed him as "one of the best known keepers in the Lighthouse Service" and mentioned his affiliation with Seattle's Nile Temple as a Shriner, confirming a story in Chapter Eight of the book.

Estelle Durgan was promoted to Semiahmoo Lighthouse Keeper following her husband's death, one of the first women to hold such a position. She died on November 4, 1943 at the age of 77.

Two of their sons, Clarence L. Durgan (born on October 21, 1889) and Edwin Lynn Durgan (born on February 9, 1898) lived in Juneau, Alaska at the time of their father's death. Lynn and his wife

Viola had seven children: Helene, Edward, Clifford, Estelle, Viola, Sally and William. He passed away on September 3, 1950.

But whatever happened to Helene Glidden? This intriguing woman lived in many places throughout Washington, Oregon and Nevada, usually by the sea or a river. Her love for the water was expressed in the many sea poems and short stories she published in *Ladies Home Journal* and *Youth's Companion* along with her two books. She also published several articles about cooking.

She originally wrote *The Light on the Island* for her own amusement, intending it for her children. Fortunately a writing instructor encouraged her to submit the manuscript for publication.

Her husband, Joseph H. Glidden, passed away on August 19, 1956, and Helene moved to Nevada the following year. Records of her whereabouts end with a 1963 cooking article published in a Honolulu newspaper. We may never know her true fate but one can assume the "little hellion" from Patos Island continued to entertain people with her escapades.

Fortunately, she recorded her musings for others to enjoy. Like all great books, the reader doesn't want *The Light on the Island* to end. This *50th Anniversary Edition* includes an Appendix with four additional stories from Mrs. Glidden's 1953 cookbook, *Pacific Coast Seafood Chef*.

While some questions may never be answered, anyone who visits Patos Island today will feel the presence of Angie, her brothers and sisters, Al, Spanish John, Mr. Blanchard, Estelle and that "fiery Frenchman" Edward LaBrege.

Michael McCloskey
March, 2001

APPENDIX

Four additional tales from Helene Glidden's cookbook, *Pacific Coast Seafood Chef,* published by Binfords & Mort (Portland, Oregon) on March 2, 1953.

SEA GULL POT PIE

S ea gulls, being scavengers, and so protected by law, are not as a rule available for food. But in the slight possibility that some of my readers may have to kill one in self-defense, I am including a recipe for Sea Gull Pot Pie.

This recipe was the result of a practical joke that backfired and turned out to be a very tempting dish.

While living on Patos Island, my parents were often visited by a famous Seattle restaurateur, who traded recipes with my mother.

On one visit, the guest noticed a flock of sea gulls hovering near the house. As he watched, a gull swooped down and snatched a slice of bread from the hand of one of the children.

"Why don't you kill them off?" asked the guest.

"They are protected," answered Mother. "I'd like to shoot a few dozen. They're an awful nuisance."

The guest smiled.

"I'd like to come by a nice big sea gull. I'd make you the finest pot pie you ever tasted. Have you ever eaten sea gull pot pie?"

"No," answered Mother. "Is it good?"

"Good? Why, there's nothing to equal its goodness. I'll make one, if you'll catch a nice big gull."

"Well, I guess one wouldn't be missed. I'll try to catch one."

Mother set a pail of kitchen scraps outside the back door and, armed with a large dip-net, she seated herself near the pail and waited.

The gulls flocked to the food. Mother singled out a gull and patiently waited for an opening. In a short time the gull waddled over near enough and Mother swooped her up in the net.

One of my brothers killed the gull and Mother plucked and cleaned it.

"Now cut it up and soak it all night in a crock filled with this solution," directed the guest. "1 quart vinegar, 2 quarts water, 2 tablespoons salt, 1 tablespoon pickling spice, 1 large onion. Boil all together and pour hot water over the gull. Let it set all night in the liquid.

Mother prepared the gull as directed, and set it on the pantry shelf to cool.

Our guest was quartered next door in my sister's side of the duplex. Late that night, when our household was sleeping, I was awakened by a soft, creeping sound downstairs. I stealthily crept to the stairway and peered over the banister. Our guest was tiptoeing out the front door with the sea gull crock in his arms. I watched as he carried it to my sister's front door. He disappeared within, and I went back to bed, wondering what he was up to.

The next morning right after breakfast he said, "Now, we'll proceed with the pot pie. Put the bird in a kettle of fresh cold water, add 1 teaspoon of soda and 1 sliced tomato. Bring it to a boil, and simmer for 2 hours."

Mother followed his directions. At the end of the specified time, our guest removed the gull from the water and stripped the flesh from his bones.

"Now, you make a good biscuit dough while I prepare the pie," he said to Mother. He went next door and returned with a bowl of sliced vegetables—carrots, potatoes, celery and onions.

"Two cups sliced carrots, 2 cups sliced potatoes, 1 cup sliced celery, 1 cup sliced onion," chanted our guest.

"Put the vegetables, by layers, in a baking dish, alternating with sea gull after each layer. Sprinkle the layers lightly with salt, pepper, $1/4$ tsp. marjoram, $1/4$ tsp. thyme. Add a little basil and rosemary leaves. Cover with the biscuit dough and bake in moderate oven for 1 hour." He worked as he talked, and soon the pie was ready for the oven.

At dinnertime, we gathered around to taste the sea gull pie.

"It's simply delicious" gurgled Mother. "Simply delicious!"

We all agreed. It was the nicest pot pie we had ever eaten. Our guest began to laugh. We were astonished at this outburst.

"Don't you find the pie tasty?" asked Mother.

"Yes I do," answered our guest, "only I must tell you the truth. This is not a gull, but chicken. I slipped the gull away during the night, and substituted a chicken. I've never cooked a gull in my life. I doubt that they are any good for food." He began to laugh again.

"Oh, my!" said Mother. "That is *very* funny. Only I'm afraid the joke is on you. You see, I watched you last night, and I recovered the sea gull from under the tank house where you hid it. You really *are* eating sea gull!"

Our guest looked rather sick for a moment. Then he shouted, "Sea gull…honest? Say this is *good*."

NIGHT FISHERMAN

I once set out to work my way through college as night operator on a switchboard in a small town whose population was largely Swedish.

This was the old Farmer's Mutual Telephone Company. The switchboards were mighty old fashioned; the type that had metal drops which flipped down, setting off a cantankerous buzzer, a persistent, angry buzz that stopped only when the drop was put back in place.

I was night operator that winter. The rule was that "central" went to bed at eleven o'clock. Any calls after that were strictly on the bonus plan, that is, any calls aside of emergencies were paid for by the caller, twenty-five cents to the operator for each call.

It was a cold winter. Many a night I had to leap out of bed, dash across a clammy concrete floor, plunk part of me in the icy chair, and say sweetly, "Number please." Then sit there until the conversation ended, so I could disconnect and put the little "flipper" back in place.

Many calls were on the up and up, and I raked in many quarters. But there were also many who "sneaked" calls. Being party lines, the subscriber merely rang her own number. When I answered, she kept silent until I replaced the drop and went back to bed. Then she could talk until exhausted and I would never know the difference. So she thought, but she was wrong. When she hung up, the little flipper *flipped*, and I had to get up to put it back in place.

Telephone operators do not as a rule listen in on conversations. In fact, there is a strict rule in telephone companies forbidding such procedure.

Because of the stolen calls, the company manager in this instance authorized the operator to supervise on any call when the subscriber refused to identify himself. It was the only means of collecting money. As a matter of fact, the farmer's lines in those days were more or less a community grapevine, and one more listener didn't matter.

So I always sat through those "sneaky calls," and *listened to every word*. If the conversation was interesting I overlooked the quarter due me. If not, I sweetly called the offenders the next morning and said, "Mrs.—, you had a call at such and such a time last night. I'm sorry, but I'll have to bill you twenty-five cents for it."

Often as not, Mrs.— didn't place the call, and indignantly shunted the blame to the real offender. That was a neat way of trapping them, though. It never failed to bring profitable results.

The Swedish people are wonderful cooks. I did a good business of night fishing. They talked for long periods while I froze the seat of my own nightgown, so I got a notebook and copied down all the recipes I heard over the telephone. I never charged a quarter to anyone from whom I got a good recipe.

Of course, I had to sift the ingredients of each recipe from the gossip that went along with it. That was sometimes hard, as the gossip often sounded like part of the ingredients. Such as "A little salt— a little spice—ja. That egg? To that ham? Oh, so full of ginger. Roll it in flour—2 cups. Rosemary. A baby! She's only been married six months. Ja. 1 cup. Baby. Brown it in oil."

Fortunately, I gathered some very tasty fish recipes such as only the Swedish people can cook. And I'm passing them on.

OCTOPUS

I t has always seemed strange to me that octopus meat has never found a large market, since the fish is so plentiful on all our rocky coasts, and is so delicious when properly prepared.

My first introduction to the tasty delicacy was the aftermath of a halibut fishing trip with Bill Coutts, my brother-in-law.

Bill had set his halibut gear one quarter mile long and we were fishing just off Sucia Island. The day was ending when Bill decided to pick up his gear. About twenty feet down below the boat on the shady side, he noticed something caught on the hooks. Then we both saw the long squirming legs of an octopus.

Bill pulled in line and quickly heaved the monster on deck, taking a turn of line about the deck cavel so he couldn't pull away.

It was uncanny the way that slithering mass of legs got around so quickly and without apparent effort. In a moment some of the legs had slid overboard and encircled the keel of the launch. Others slid up over the pilot house, two encircled the smokestack. I crouched in terrified fascination from my stronghold in the engine room.

Bill had on rubber boots. The octopus wrapped two legs around them. I could see the huge cups, like morning glories, as they sucked around Bill's legs.

"The ax," he shouted.

I handed it out to him. He was glued to the spot.

The legs were all of eight feet long. Bill chopped at the base of them, which measured about 3½ inches in diameter. He severed one leg. As he chopped, I noticed the whip-like end thrashing in a snaky manner.

In a moment the encircling legs were both severed, but with a graceful movement the octopus had withdrawn one of the others from the smokestack and was coiling it around Bill. Quickly, Bill smashed the ax into the monster's owl-like face.

After he disentangled all eight legs, Bill chopped them into short pieces, skinned them and put the lovely white meat into the tub.

He recovered his gear and we returned home.

Mother was skeptical about the meat being good for food, but Bill pounded some, rolled it in cracker crumbs and eggs, and fried it. We all tasted and judged it excellent. Octopus soon became a favorite family dish.

It may be fried or boiled for chowder. We frequently broiled pieces over hot coals, a very delicious method of cooking it.

To prepare octopus for cooking, plunge the pieces of leg in boiling water for 1 minute. Remove and skin. Pound with a steak pounder. Either fry like a fillet of sole, or put through food chopper and use for chowder or casserole dishes.

PUGET SOUND CLAM CHOWDER

This chowder recipe at one time brought fame to a certain hotel chef because of one of my escapades.

When my father was appointed keeper at Semiahmoo Harbor light station, which is located one mile off shore from Blaine, Washington, he established a home in the town for our family. I was about fourteen.

While talking myself out of the many difficulties I encountered during the process of becoming "civilized," I informed the populace about a fabulous island whence I had come.

Of course, my school friends were greatly interested, and I promised several of them that I'd take them to the island at the first opportunity.

My especial hobby had always been boats, and one day when I was cruising about Semiahmoo Harbor in my launch, which was a reconverted lighthouse lifeboat, I noticed a strange steamer lying at one of the piers. I ran alongside of her and engaged the deck hand in conversation. He became interested in my boat and climbed down to examine the engine. We talked awhile, and he gave me permission to board the steamer. While I was being shown through, the skipper, Captain Lindsey, came aboard. In a few minutes I was chatting with him about boats, lighthouses and Patos Island.

"I've been there," he said. "I've taken several excursions to Patos."

"What's an excursion?" I asked.

"That's where you take a lot of people on a trip and bring them back," he informed me.

"Oh, will you take my friends to Patos?" I asked.

"If there are over fifty of them," he answered. "I won't go for less than fifty."

That sounded wonderful to me. I couldn't believe my good fortune. I had been trying to find a way to take my friends to Patos, and now this good captain was offering to take them all, and more too.

"Oh, I can arrange to get more than fifty to go," I answered. "I'll get sixty-five."

"All right," he said. "I'll go for sixty-five. You do the collecting, and I'll go a week from Sunday. I'll give you sixty-five tickets." He gave me the tickets, which read *Excursion Cruise Steamer San Juan*. We filled in the date and the hour in pencil.

The next day I quickly passed the tickets out all over town.

On Saturday morning, the day before the excursion, Father came rushing into the house. "Where's that damn Annie?" he roared. Father was a fiery Frenchman and when aroused was quite profane.

"Why, what's wrong?" asked Mother.

I remained concealed behind the pantry door, wondering whether or not I had properly moored the launch on the previous day. That was usually the thing that infuriated Father. I often forgot to make secure the stern line, and the boat had once swung around on the piling, damaging the propeller blades.

"Wrong!" shouted Father. "Why, that little hellion has engaged the *San Juan* for an excursion to Patos tomorrow. And Captain Lindsey asked me for the sixty-five dollars this morning!"

I staggered out of the pantry.

"Sixty-five dollars?" I gasped.

My mouth was frozen open, because I remember Mother coming over to me and gently closing it.

Father swung around and faced me.

"What in—did you do it for?" he yelled.

"I didn't know it cost anything!" I shouted back, and then burst out crying. That's the way you had to handle Father. You matched his anger and then resorted to tears. Father was a pushover for tears.

He threw both hands above his head and groaned; then, clapping them over his forehead, he ran into the living room, followed by Mother.

In a few minutes Mother came out. I was sitting, still stunned, at the kitchen table, trying to figure out what had happened.

"Anne," Mother began, "could you gather up those sixty-five tickets?" Before I could tell her that I gave them out indiscriminately, and had no idea who had them all, Father came in.

"It's no use," he said. "The tickets are out. The boat is engaged. We have to make it good, or the skipper will be out the money. He reserved the day for Anne, and his company would hold him accountable for the lost excursion."

"What shall we do?" asked Mother.

"We could collect the fares at the dock," said father, "but that may not work out." A lot of folks might back out when they learn they have to pay one dollar."

"I think that Anne needs a good lesson. She's always getting us into this sort of thing." Mother's blue eyes were cold and gray. She continued, "These escapades have to stop. It was only a few months ago that she engaged the main dining room at the Leopold in Bellingham for a birthday party for Governor Lister. That cost us four hundred dollars."

"Yes," agreed Father. "I am still smarting over the financial beating I took when she hired three sleighs from the livery stable, so she could take her friends for a sleigh ride."

"She has no idea of the meaning of money," said Mother, "and I intend to teach her right now. She will have to pay for this excursion herself."

She turned to me. "You find yourself some sort of work after school," she said. "Perhaps you can wash dishes or tend some-one's baby."

After Father left, I sat and brooded over my fate. If I had to work after school, there would be no time for the much-loved boat rides around the harbor. Life looked very dark indeed.

The phone rang. It was one of Mother's friends asking for Father's clam chowder recipe.

"You really should set up a little tea room and sell clam chowder," she said. "I've *never* tasted anything quite so delicious!"

After she hung up, I had a bright idea. Why couldn't I make clam chowder and sell it to the excursionists on Sunday?

I found Mother and outlined my plan to her.

"It *could* be done, if you could get enough clams," she agreed. "But is there enough time to get things together?"

"I'll get help," I shouted. The door slammed behind me as I ran out.

The rest of the day, two neighbor boys and I dug and hauled three gunnysacks full of geoducks all the way from Semiahmoo Spit mud flats to the pier where the *San Juan* was tied up.

After an agreement with Captain Lindsey, we put the clams aboard to soak in three galvanized tubs.

In early evening I made arrangements with our grocer for salt pork, celery, bacon, and crackers. I traded him several sacks of homegrown potatoes for the groceries. We had plenty of carrots and onions in our own garden.

Late that night, I had everything aboard the steamer. I was tired, afraid, and near tears. Tomorrow's work loomed before me dark and dismal.

I boarded the *San Juan* very early Sunday morning. The work of cleaning clams, cutting up all the vegetables, and making the chowder seemed a gigantic task. Mother refused to help.

When I opened the door to the galley, there was Father, in apron and cap.

"Father!" I cried.

"Did you think I'd let you down, *petite*?" he crooned, while I cried in his arms. "We'll do this thing up in our best French style. You and me."

All that day I peeled and cut into cubes potatoes and onions, cleaned and cut up carrots and celery, bacon, salt pork, and clams.

In the midst of it all, when the clam slime was running down my arms to drip off my elbows, and my eyes and nose were dripping from the onions, the galley door opened and in came the boy I'd been trying to attract for many long months. He took one look at me shouted, "For gosh sakes, don't let that running nose drip in the soup."

By lunchtime I had cut into cubes four pounds of salt pork, four pounds of bacon, forty cups of potatoes, sixteen cups of carrots, sixteen cups of onion, eight cups of celery, thirty-two quarts of clams.

The chowder was done, and we began to serve it. We charged twenty cents a plate. We had planned to serve only one helping at noon, and have the rest on our return trip during the evening, but the passengers kept returning for seconds. Father made a quick computation.

"If we sell it all, you'll have twenty-six dollars," he said.

There was one man I noticed, who kept coming back. He was a funny little short fellow, with handlebar mustaches, and black darting eyes. As he ate the chowder, he seemed to be picking it apart in his spoon, as if hunting for something. After each spoonful, he'd screw up his lips and make a little sound, half smack and half sucking. Fascinated, I watched him eat. After each smack, he'd look up with a quizzical frown.

One of the passengers asked me for the recipe for the chowder. Father said that I might take her name down and mail the recipe to her for ten cents, plus postage. In a few minutes I was taking names as fast as I could write. Everyone seemed to want the recipe. At ten cents apiece I would make about six dollars more. Not even half of the required amount to pay for the boat.

The funny little lip-smacking man came into the galley. He pointed at Father.

"I'll go crazy!" he said. "I eat and eat. I don't find that certain taste out... what you put in?"

"If you want the recipe," answered Father, "give your name to Anne, like all the rest. She'll mail it to you."

The little man came over to me and looked at the long list of names.

"All these people recipe wanting?" he asked.

"Yes," I answered. "Shall I put your name down?"

He turned to Father.

"Stop!" he cried. "Don't recipe give. I pay you for it . . . good. I pay you three hundred dolla for it. You tell all these people to come to Manuel at the Border Hotel. I make it for them. I make money, you make money. Chowder no more you make."

"Sold!" shouted Father, and he shook hands with Manuel.

"What's in it?" asked Manuel.

"That's a secret," said Father. "A French secret. It's rosemary and basil."

The little man grabbed his stomach and laughed.

"*Mi Dios*! Three hundred dolla for herbs!"

PUGET SOUND CLAM CHOWDER
(Three Hundred Dollar Recipe)

$1/4$ lb. diced salt pork
$1/4$ lb. diced bacon
$2^1/2$ cups diced raw potatoes
1 cup diced onion
1 cup diced carrots
$1/2$ cup diced celery
$1/2$ clove chopped garlic
Small piece bay leaf
$1/4$ tsp. rosemary (crushed)
$1/4$ tsp. basil (crushed)
$1^1/2$ tsp. thyme
3 peppercorns
$1^1/2$ tsp. salt
1 qt. chopped clams
Clam liquor and water, 1 qt.
1 tbsp. Worcestershire Sauce

Brown bacon and pork until crisp. Carefully fry onions until delicately browned. Add vegetables and garlic, cover and simmer for 10 minutes. Add seasonings. Add liquor and water, clams. Cook gently until vegetables are done. Add 1 qt. rich milk or cream.

ORDERING INFORMATION

Also available from San Juan Publishing:

Once Upon an Island by David Conover
Andrew Henry's Meadow by Doris Burn
Springer's Journey by Naomi Black and Virginia Heaven
Gloria's Miracle by Jerry Brewer

San Juan Publishing
P.O. Box 923
Woodinville, WA 98072
425-485-2813
sanjuanbooks@yahoo.com